MW01027002

Great Expectations
- a stage play

Adapted by

John R. Goodman

from the novel by Charles Dickens

To enquire about performance rights for this play, please go to
https://johnrgoodman.com/contact/

Rights are normally granted free to educational
and community groups; a donation at
https://progresstheatre.co.uk/fundraising
is appreciated.

Introduction

I had long had a hankering to direct a classic novel for the stage and Dickens seemed an obvious place to start. Charles Dickens himself was an enthusiast for theatre, sometimes taking to the stage himself. His novels are full of incident and emotion, with memorable characters, protagonists and antagonists, and shot through with humour. His works lend themselves to drama and many talented writers have adapted them for both stage and screen, over many years.

Without doubt, *A Christmas Carol* is the most frequently adapted of his works. It is short enough to turn into a film or a stage play without sacrificing major plot points. Dickens' longer novels present more of a challenge, and perhaps that is why I could not settle on an existing stage adaptation of *Great Expectations* that completely satisfied me. My main reservations were two-fold. First, too many elements of the story would be cut from the script. For instance, the subplot involving Orlick was often deleted, but this would lead to hanging threads elsewhere: with no Orlick, we are left to wonder what exactly became of Mrs Joe.

My second issue with other scripts was with the dialogue. Dickens wrote wonderful dialogue that defined the personality of his characters, bringing out their eccentricity and comic traits. It is presumptuous for an adapter to decide they can improve upon conversations written by Charles Dickens. Of course, much of it can sound anachronistic, and he used a lot of repetition for comic effect, but his words are a lot more accessible to modern ears than Shakespeare.

So, I set out to add to the numerous adaptations of *Great Expectations*. Surely, all I had to do was delete anything that wasn't a conversation, making sure what remained told the story? But of course, that still left far too much to make a stage play. So it was necessary to kill off characters. One sad loss was Mr Wopsle – the star of a chapter that may be the funniest in the novel, but a chapter that contained no dialogue. His friend Pumblechook remains in a much-reduced role. Another unlucky victim of cuts was The Aged Parent – Wemmick's elderly father. The scenes at the Wemmick home in Walworth are charming, but can hardly be said to advance the plot. Herbert's family and fiancée also fell by the wayside, along with the various hangers-on at Miss Havisham's house. Despite these excisions, the script is faithful to the main plot of the novel, with no original dialogue. Charles Dickens wrote every word spoken by the actors.

Dickens at first wrote a more downbeat ending to *Great Expectations*, but another writer persuaded him to change it to a more optimistic tone. However, he expresses this optimism in prose, not in the dialogue, so the ending in this play is more ambiguous. It is for the director and audience to speculate what happiness Pip's future may hold. Speaking of Pip, spare a thought for the lead actor: a consequence of adapting a novel written in the first person is that Pip is central to every scene and so never leaves the stage.

This should be a useful script for anybody studying the novel. It condenses the 183,000 odd words of the original to something less than 23,000: an evening's worth of theatre. Hopefully, it also provides a fast-moving and entertaining version of Pip's story. Enjoy!

John R. Goodman

Characters

PIP — an orphan child, grows to adulthood

MAGWITCH — escaped convict, strong.

JOE GARGERY — a blacksmith

MRS JOE — wife to Joe and Pip's much older sister

PUMBLECHOOK — uncle to Joe, local corn merchant

COMPEYSON — another convict

SERGEANT — in pursuit of escaped convicts

SOLDIERS — 2 or more

ESTELLA — Miss Havisham's ward, grows to adulthood

MISS HAVISHAM — a reclusive spinster

HERBERT POCKET — young cousin to Miss Havisham, grows to adulthood

JAGGERS — a lawyer

WEMMICK — clerk to Jaggers

ORLICK — journeyman blacksmith

MOLLY — servant to Jaggers

DRUMMLE — sulky companion to Herbert and Pip

BIDDY — a young friend of Pip's

WATCHMAN

OFFICER

JUDGE

Produced by Progress Theatre in July 2022 in the open air at Reading Abbey Ruins, with the following cast.

Dean Stephenson	Pip
Peter Knightley	Magwitch
Paul Gittus	Joe, Judge
Juliet England	Mrs Joe, Molly
Peter Cook	Jaggers, Pumblechook
Mikhail Franklin	Compeyson, Orlick
Assunta Palladio	Sergeant, Servant
Jackson Dale	Wemmick, Soldier
Ethan Law	Drummle, Soldier
Nancy Gittus	Biddy
Evie Stonehouse	Estella
Ali Carroll	Miss Havisham
Dylan Collie	Herbert
Lauren Boys	Watchman, Waiter

ACT ONE

Scene 1. A graveyard.

Shrouded in mist, an outsize headstone carved with

Phillip Pirrip
Also Georgiana,
Wife of the above

PIP, as a boy, enters, looking around nervously. He approaches the headstone and traces some of the letters with a finger. He sniffs, then sits with his back to the headstone, puts his head in his hands and sobs. The sound of a cannon and MAGWITCH, an escaped convict in a leg iron, rears up from behind the headstone.

MAGWITCH. Hold your noise!

PIP tries to run. MAGWITCH Grabs him.

MAGWITCH.   Keep still, you little devil, or I'll cut your throat!

PIP.   Oh! Don't cut my throat, sir! Pray, don't do it, sir!

MAGWITCH.   Tell us your name! Quick!

PIP. Pip, sir.

MAGWITCH.   Once more, give it mouth!

PIP.   Pip. Pip, sir.

MAGWITCH.   Show us where you live. Pint out the place!

PIP slowly raises an arm and points off stage. MAGWITCH picks him up and turns him upside down. A piece of bread falls out of a pocket which MAGWITCH grabs and eats hungrily.

MAGWITCH.   You young dog, what cheeks you ha' got. Darn Me if I couldn't eat 'em!

PIP.   I hope you would not, sir.

MAGWITCH.   Now look'ee here! Where's your mother?

PIP.   There, sir!

PIP points at the headstone. MAGWITCH starts to run, stops, looks at headstone.

PIP.   There, sir! Also Georgiana. That's my mother.

MAGWITCH.   Oh! And is that your father alonger your mother?

PIP.   Yes, sir, him too; late of this parish.

MAGWITCH.   Ha! Who d'ye live with—supposin' you're kindly let to live, which I han't made up my mind about?

PIP.   My sister, sir—Mrs. Joe Gargery—wife of Joe Gargery, the blacksmith, sir.

MAGWITCH.   Blacksmith, eh? Now look'ee here, you know what a file is?

PIP.   Yes, sir.

MAGWITCH.   And you know what wittles is?

PIP.   Yes, sir. [*mimes eating*]

MAGWITCH [*grabbing PIP and tilting him*].   You get me a file. And you get me wittles. You bring 'em both to me. Or I'll have your heart and liver out.

PIP.   If you would kindly please to let me keep upright, sir, perhaps I shouldn't be sick, and perhaps I could attend more.

MAGWITCH. You bring me, tomorrow morning early, that file and them wittles. And you never say a word concerning your having seen such a person as me, and you shall be let to live. You fail, and your heart and your liver shall be tore out, roasted, and ate. Now, I ain't alone. There's a young man hid with me, in comparison with which I am a Angel. That young man has a secret way of getting at a boy, and at his heart, and at his liver. A boy may be warm in bed, may tuck himself up, but that young man will softly creep his way to him and tear him open. I am a keeping that young man from harming of you with great difficulty. I find it wery hard to hold him off of your inside. Now, what do you say?

PIP. I'll bring the file tomorrow, sir. And what wittles I can get.

MAGWITCH. Say, Lord strike you dead if you don't!

PIP. Lord strike me dead if I don't.

MAGWITCH [*Gazing at the surrounding marsh*]. I wish I was a frog. Or a eel.

MAGWITCH exits, limping. PIP runs home, to find...

Scene 2. Gargery kitchen

JOE Gargery, a blacksmith, sitting in the kitchen.

JOE. Mrs. Joe has been out a dozen times, looking for you, Pip. And she's out now, making it a baker's dozen.

PIP. Is she?

JOE. Yes, Pip, and what's worse, she's got Tickler with

her. She Ram-paged out. She's a coming!

MRS JOE enters, carrying a cane (Tickler). She beats PIP and throws him at JOE, who shields him.

MRS JOE.   Where have you been, you young monkey? Tell me directly what you've been doing to wear me away with fret and fright and worrit, or I'd have you out of that corner if you was fifty Pips, and he was five hundred Gargerys.

PIP.   I have only been to the churchyard.

MRS JOE.   Churchyard! If it warn't for me you'd have been to the churchyard long ago, and stayed there. Who brought you up by hand?

PIP.   You did.

MRS JOE.   And why did I do it, I should like to know?

PIP.   I don't know.

MRS JOE.   I don't! I'd never do it again! I know that. Hah! Churchyard, indeed! You'll drive me to the churchyard betwixt you, one of these days, and O, a pr-r-recious pair you'd be without me!

MRS JOE begins slicing and buttering bread, aggressively. Joe passes a slice to PIP and takes one for himself.

The sound of a distant cannon.

PIP.   Hark! was that the great guns, Joe?

JOE.   There's another conwict off.

PIP.   What does that mean, Joe?

MRS JOE.   Escaped. Escaped.

PIP.   What's a convict?

MRS JOE. Drat that boy, what a questioner he is. Ask no questions, and you'll be told no lies.

The guns sound again. Unseen by the others, PIP stuffs his bread into his clothing.

PIP. Mrs. Joe, I should like to know—if you wouldn't much mind—where the firing comes from?

MRS JOE. Lord bless the boy! From the Hulks!

PIP. And please, what's Hulks?

MRS JOE. That's the way with this boy! Answer him one question, and he'll ask you a dozen directly. Hulks are prison-ships, right 'cross th' marshes.

PIP. I wonder who's put into prison-ships, and why they're put there?

MRS JOE. I didn't bring you up by hand to badger people's lives out. People are put in the Hulks because they murder, and because they rob, and forge, and do all sorts of bad; and they always begin by asking questions. Now, you get along to bed!

PIP goes to his bed. Joe and Mrs Joe clear away the supper and leave.

A clock strikes five and it is first light, but still dim.

PIP creeps into the kitchen and takes a pie, some bread and cheese, and decants some brandy into a small glass bottle.

Eerie voices whisper, "Get up, Mrs Joe!" and "Stop thief!".

Pip goes off and returns with a file from the forge, gathering everything into a cloth, he runs for the misty marshes.

Scene 3. The marshes.

As he runs through the marshes the voices continue: "A boy with somebody else's pork pie! Stop him!" An ox lows and speaks: "Halloa, young thief"!

PIP: I couldn't help it, sir! It wasn't for myself I took it!

He runs on. A man (COMPEYSON) dressed as a convict and also wearing a leg iron appears, slouched over on the ground. PIP touches him on the shoulder and is shocked to see it is not his convict. The man roars and takes a swing at PIP who dodges. The man stumbles away.

PIP: It's the young man!

PIP runs on until he runs into MAGWITCH, who is shivering and limping. He sits on the ground as PIP opens his bundle.

MAGWITCH. What's in the bottle, boy?

PIP. Brandy.

MAGWITCH hurriedly gobbles the food, shivering. He pauses to take some of the brandy.

PIP. I think you have got the ague.

MAGWITCH. I'm much of your opinion, boy.

PIP. It's bad about here. You've been lying out on the meshes, and they're dreadful ague-ish.

MAGWITCH. I'll eat my breakfast afore they're the death of me. [*takes another mouthful, then grabs Pip*] You're not a deceiving imp? You brought no one with you?

PIP. No, sir. No!

MAGWITCH. Nor giv' no one the office to follow you?

PIP. No!

MAGWITCH [*releasing PIP*]. Well, I believe you. You'd be but a fierce young hound indeed, if you could help to hunt a wretched warmint hunted as near death and dunghill as this poor wretched warmint is!

PIP. I am afraid you won't leave any of it for him.

MAGWITCH. Leave any for him? Who's him?

PIP. The young man. That you spoke of. That was hid with you.

MAGWITCH. Him? Yes, yes! He don't want no wittles.

PIP. I thought he looked as if he did.

MAGWITCH. Looked? When?

PIP. Just now.

MAGWITCH. Where?

PIP. Yonder, over there, where I found him, and thought it was you.

MAGWITCH grabs PIP by the collar and stares at him.

PIP. Dressed like you—and with—the same reason for wanting to borrow a file. Didn't you hear the cannon last night?

MAGWITCH. Then there was firing!

PIP. I wonder you shouldn't have been sure of that, for we heard it up at home.

MAGWITCH. Why, see now! When a man's alone on these flats, he hears nothin' but guns firing, and voices calling. Hears? He sees the soldiers, with their red coats closing in round him. But this man - where is he? I'll pull him down, like a bloodhound. Curse this iron on my leg! Give us hold of the file, boy.

MAGWITCH files at his iron like a madman. PIP watches for a moment, then turns and runs home.

Scene 4. Gargery kitchen

Offstage, cast singing "God Rest Ye Merry Gentlemen".

MRS JOE. And where the deuce ha' you been?

PIP. Down to hear the carols.

MRS JOE. Ah! Well! You might ha' done worse.

Enter Pumblechook, with bottles.

MRS JOE. O, Un—cle Pum-ble—chook! Merry Christmas! This is kind!

PUMBLECHOOK. It's no more than your merits. Compliments of the season!

MRS JOE. All is ready, Uncle.

All bow their heads.

PUMBLECHOOK. For these festive blessings which we are about to receive, may the Good Lord make us truly grateful.

ALL. Amen.

Everybody takes their seat and Joe serves out food.

MRS JOE. Do you hear that? Be grateful.

PUMBLECHOOK. Especially be grateful, boy, to them which brought you up by hand.

MRS JOE. We must taste, to begin with, such a delightful and delicious present of Uncle Pumblechook's!

PIP looks alarmed.

MRS JOE. You must know, it's a pie, a savoury pork pie.

She goes to fetch it. PIP bows his head.

JOE. A bit of pork pie would lay atop of anything you could mention, and do no harm.

MRS JOE re-enters, empty-handed.

MRS JOE. Gracious goodness gracious me, what's gone—the pie!

PIP runs to the door, just as the SERGEANT steps through and places one hand on PIP's shoulder, with a pair of handcuffs in the other. A soldier follows him in. PIP gasps.

SERGEANT. Excuse me, ladies and gentlemen, but I am on a chase in the name of the king, and I want the blacksmith.

MRS JOE. And pray what might you want with him?

SERGEANT. Missis, speaking for myself, I should reply, the honour and pleasure of his fine wife's acquaintance; speaking for the king, I answer, a little job done. You see, blacksmith, we have had an accident with these. Will you throw your eye over them?

JOE examines the handcuffs, nods and takes them off into the forge. The sound of hammering.

SERGEANT. How far might you call yourselves from the marshes? Not above a mile, I reckon?

PUMBLECHOOK. Just a mile. Convicts, sergeant?

SERGEANT. Two. They're pretty well known to be out on the marshes still, and they won't try to get clear of 'em before dusk. Anybody here seen anything of any such game?

ADULTS. No.

Joe returns with the handcuffs.

JOE. Pip and I will alonger the soldiers and see what comes of the hunt.

Pip tries to hide his distress.

MRS JOE. If you bring the boy back with his head blown to bits by a musket, don't look to me to put it together again!

Scene 5. The marshes.

JOE and PIP follow the SERGEANT and SOLDIERS through the marshes.

SERGEANT [*to JOE and PIP*]. Keep in the rear and speak no word!

PIP [*Whispers*]. I hope, Joe, we shan't find them.

JOE. I'd give a shilling if they had cut and run, Pip.

In the distance, a shout.

SERGEANT. At the double!

SERGEANT and SOLDIERS run on. They find

MAGWITCH and COMPEYSON fighting.

SERGEANT. Surrender, you two! and confound you for wild beasts!

SOLDIERS separate and apprehend the two convicts.

MAGWITCH. I took him! I give him up to you! Mind that!

COMPEYSON. Take notice, guard, —he tried to murder me!

MAGWITCH. I took him, and giv' him up. Single-handed I got clear of the prison-ship. I could ha' got clear of these death-cold flats likewise, if I hadn't made the discovery that he was here.

COMPEYSON. Didn't I tell you, that he would murder me, if he could?

SERGEANT. Enough of this parley. March!

MAGWITCH. I wish to say something respecting this escape. It may prevent some persons laying under suspicion alonger me. A man can't starve. I took some wittles, up at the willage over yonder.

SERGEANT. You mean stole.

MAGWITCH. And I'll tell you where from. From the blacksmith's.

JOE. Halloa, Pip!

MAGWITCH. It was some wittles—a dram of liquor, and a pie.

SERGEANT. Have you happened to miss such an article as a pie, blacksmith?

JOE. My wife did, at the very moment when you came in.

MAGWITCH. So, you're the blacksmith? Than I'm sorry to say, I've et your pie.

JOE. God knows you're welcome to it. We don't know what you have done, but we wouldn't have you starved to death for it, poor miserable fellow-creatur. —Would us, Pip?

SERGEANT and SOLDIERS escort the convicts off.

Scene 6. Gargery kitchen.

PIP and another child, BIDDY, are giggling over a slate, on which she is helping him to write. PIP gives the slate to JOE.

JOE. I say, Pip, old chap! What a scholar you are! An't you?

PIP. I should like to be. Biddy has been teaching me.

BIDDY smiles, shyly.

JOE. Which she is a clever friend to you. Why, here's a J and a O equal to anythink! Here's a J and a O, Joe.

PIP. How do you spell Gargery, Joe?

JOE. I don't spell it at all.

PIP. But supposing you did?

JOE. It can't be supposed.

PIP. Didn't you ever go to school, Joe, when you were as little as me?

JOE. No, Pip.

PIP. Why didn't you go to school, Joe?

JOE. I'll tell you. My father, Pip, he were given to drink, and he hammered away at my mother and me with a wigor only to be equalled by the wigor with which he didn't hammer at his anwil. So, I went to work at my present calling, and I worked tolerable hard, Pip. In time I were able to keep him, till he went off in a purple leptic fit. Which, you see, Pip, were a drawback on my learning.

PIP/BIDDY. Poor Joe.

JOE. It were but lonesome then. When I got acquainted with your sister, it were the talk how she was bringing you up by hand. I said to her, 'And bring the poor little child, there's room for him at the forge!'

PIP cries and throws his arms around JOE's neck. BIDDY, smiling, exits with the slate.

JOE. Ever the best of friends; an't us, Pip? Don't cry, old chap!

Enter MRS JOE and PUMBLECHOOK.

MRS JOE. Now, if this boy ain't grateful this night, he never will be! It's only to be hoped that he won't be Pompeyed.

PUMBLECHOOK. She ain't in that line, Mum. She knows better.

JOE. She? She?

MRS JOE. And she is a she, I suppose? Unless you call Miss Havisham a he.

JOE. Miss Havisham, up town?

MRS JOE. Is there any Miss Havisham down town? She wants this boy to go and play there. And he had better play there, or I'll work him.

MRS JOE begins scrubbing PIP's face and changing him into his Sunday best.

JOE. I wonder how she come to know Pip!

MRS JOE. Noodle! Who said she knew him?

JOE. Which some individual mentioned that she wanted him to go and play there.

MRS JOE. And couldn't she ask Uncle Pumblechook if he knew of a boy to go and play there? Isn't it possible that Uncle Pumblechook be a tenant of hers, and that he sometimes go there to pay his rent? And couldn't she then ask Uncle Pumblechook if he knew a boy? And couldn't Uncle Pumblechook then mention this boy, standing Prancing here that I have for ever been a willing slave to?

PUMBLECHOOK. Well put! Prettily pointed! Good indeed! Now Joseph, you know the case.

MRS JOE. No, Joseph, you do not yet know the case. For you do not know that Uncle Pumblechook has offered to take him in his own cart, to Miss Havisham's. And Lor-a-mussy me! Here I stand talking to mere Mooncalfs, with Uncle Pumblechook waiting!

PUMBLECHOOK. Boy, be forever grateful to all friends, but especially unto them which brought you up by hand!

PIP. Good-bye, Joe!

JOE. God bless you, Pip, old chap!

Scene 7. Satis House gate

PUMBLECHOOK and PIP approach the gate of Satis House. ESTELLA is behind it, or just offstage. PUMBLECHOOK rings a bell pull.

ESTELLA. What name?

PUMBLECHOOK. Pumblechook.

ESTELLA. Quite right!

ESTELLA enters with a large set of keys and unlocks the gate.

PUMBLECHOOK. This is Pip.

ESTELLA. This is Pip, is it? Come in, Pip.

PUMBLECHOOK starts to enter. ESTELLA stops him.

ESTELLA. Oh! Did you wish to see Miss Havisham?

PUMBLECHOOK. If Miss Havisham wished to see me.

ESTELLA. Ah! But you see she don't.

PUMBLECHOOK. Boy! Let your behaviour be a credit to them which brought you up by hand!

She locks the gate and PUMBLECHOOK exits. PIP follows her.

Scene 8. Satis House.

ESTELLA leads PIP on a winding route through the darkened house.

PIP. What is the name of this house, miss?

ESTELLA. Its name is Satis, which is Greek, or Latin, for enough.

PIP. Enough House; that's a curious name, miss.

ESTELLA. It meant, that whoever had this house could want nothing else. They must have been easily satisfied in those days, I should think. But don't loiter, boy. Go in.

PIP. After you, miss.

ESTELLA. Don't be ridiculous, boy; I am not going in.

She walks away. We hear PIP knock.

HAVISHAM. Enter!

Miss HAVISHAM, seated at a dressing table. She is dressed in a faded wedding dress, with a veil and just one white shoe. A clock is stopped at twenty to nine.

HAVISHAM. Who is it?

PIP. Pip, ma'am. Mr. Pumblechook's boy, come to play.

HAVISHAM. Come; let me look at you. You are not afraid of a woman who has never seen the sun since you were born?

PIP [*afraid*]. No.

HAVISHAM. Do you know what I touch here?

PIP. Yes, ma'am. Your heart.

HAVISHAM. Broken! [*Beat*] I am tired. I want diversion. Play. I have a sick fancy that I want to see some play. There, there! Play, play, play!

Pause. PIP is confused.

HAVISHAM. Are you sullen and obstinate?

PIP. No, ma'am, I am very sorry I can't play just now. If you complain of me, I shall get into trouble with my sister; but it's so new here, and so strange... and melancholy...

HAVISHAM. So new to him, so old to me; so strange to him, so familiar to me; so melancholy to both of us! Call Estella. At the door.

Great Expectations – a stage play

PIP steps out.

PIP. Estella!

ESTELLA approaches with her candle, which she lifts to PIP's face. She scoffs and together they return to the candlelit room. Miss HAVISHAM takes a jewel from the dressing table and holds it up to ESTELLA's breast.

HAVISHAM. Your own, one day, my dear. Let me see you play cards with this boy.

ESTELLA. With this boy? Why, he is a common labouring boy!

HAVISHAM. Well? You can break his heart.

ESTELLA. What do you play, boy?

PIP. Nothing but beggar my neighbour, miss.

HAVISHAM. Beggar him.

They play cards on the floor as Miss HAVISHAM watches.

ESTELLA. Queen.

PIP plays two cards.

PIP. Jack!

ESTELLA. He calls the knaves Jacks, this boy! And what coarse hands he has! And what thick boots!

PIP nervously drops his cards.

ESTELLA. Stupid, clumsy labouring-boy!

HAVISHAM. You say nothing of her. She says many hard things of you, but you say nothing of her. What do you think of her?

PIP. I don't like to say.

HAVISHAM. Tell me in my ear.

PIP. I think she is very proud

HAVISHAM. Anything else?

PIP. I think she is very pretty.

HAVISHAM. Anything else?

PIP. I think she is very insulting.

HAVISHAM. Anything else?

PIP. I think I should like to go home.

HAVISHAM. And never see her again, though she is so pretty?

PIP. I am not sure I shouldn't like to see her again, but I should like to go home now.

HAVISHAM. When shall I have you here again? Come again after six days. You hear?

PIP. Yes, ma'am.

HAVISHAM. Estella, take him down. Let him roam and look about before he leaves. Go, Pip.

PIP, stumbling, stifles a sob and follows ESTELLA and her candle through the dark house to...

Scene 9. Satis House gate.

ESTELLA. You are to wait here, you boy. Why don't you cry?

PIP. Because I don't want to.

ESTELLA. You do. You have been crying till you are half

22

blind, and you are near crying again now.

She exits. Enter HERBERT Pocket, as a boy.

HERBERT. Who let you in?

PIP. Miss Estella.

HERBERT. Who gave you leave to prowl about?

PIP. Miss Havisham.

HERBERT. Come and fight. Stop a minute, though. I ought to give you a reason for fighting, too. There it is.

HERBERT slaps PIP and pulls his hair. He dances about like a boxer, fists raised.

HERBERT. Laws of the game! Regular rules!

They fight and HERBERT is knocked down. He gets up and is knocked down again.

HERBERT. That means you have won.

PIP. Can I help you?

HERBERT. No thankee.

PIP. Good afternoon

HERBERT. Same to you.

HERBERT exits. Estella returns.

ESTELLA. Come here! You may kiss me, if you like.

Pip kisses her cheek. She unlocks the gate and ushers him out.

Scene 10. Gargery kitchen

PUMBLECHOOK. Well, boy, how did you get on up town?

PIP. Pretty well, sir.

MRS. JOE launches herself at PIP with a cry.
PUMBLECHOOK intervenes.

PUMBLECHOOK. No! Don't lose your temper. Leave this lad to me, ma'am; leave this lad to me. Boy! What like is Miss Havisham?

PIP. Very tall and dark.

MRS JOE. Is she, uncle?

PUMBLECHOOK nods vaguely.

PUMBLECHOOK. This is the way to have him, I think, Mum!

MRS JOE. Uncle, you know so well how to deal with him.

PUMBLECHOOK. Now, boy! What was she a doing of, when you went in today?

PIP. She was sitting in a black velvet coach.

MRS JOE. In a black velvet coach?

PIP. Yes, and Miss Estella—that's her niece, I think—handed her in cake and wine at the coach-window, on a gold plate. And we all had cake and wine. And I got up behind the coach to eat mine, because she told me to.

PUMBLECHOOK. Was anybody else there?

PIP. Four dogs.

PUMBLECHOOK. Large or small?

PIP. Immense, and they fought for veal-cutlets out of a

silver basket.

MRS JOE.   Where was this coach, in the name of gracious?

PIP.   In Miss Havisham's room. But there weren't any horses to it.

MRS JOE.   Can this be possible, uncle?

PUMBLECHOOK.   I'll tell you, Mum. My opinion is, it's a sedan-chair. She's quite flighty enough to pass her days in a sedan-chair.

MRS JOE.   Did you ever see her in it, uncle?

PUMBLECHOOK.   How could I, when I never see her in my life? Never clapped eyes upon her!

MRS JOE.   Goodness, uncle! And yet you have spoken to her?

PUMBLECHOOK.   Why, don't you know that when I have been there, I have been took up to the outside of her door, and the door has stood ajar, and she has spoke to me that way.

Scene 11. Joe's forge

Joe is at his anvil.

PIP.   Joe, I should like to tell you something.

JOE.   Should you, Pip? Then tell us. What is it, Pip?

PIP.   Joe, you heard all that about Miss Havisham's?

JOE.   Wonderful!

PIP.   It's a terrible thing, Joe; it ain't true.

JOE. What are you telling of, Pip? You don't mean to say it's—

PIP. Yes I do; it's lies, Joe.

JOE. But not all of it? Why sure you don't mean to say, Pip, that there was no black welwet co—eh? But at least there was dogs, Pip? Come, Pip, if there warn't no weal-cutlets, at least there was dogs?

PIP. No, Joe.

JOE. A dog? A puppy?

PIP. No, Joe, there was nothing at all of the kind.

JOE. Pip, old chap! This won't do, old fellow! I say! Where do you expect to go to?

PIP. It's terrible, Joe; ain't it?

JOE. Terrible? Awful! What possessed you?

PIP. [*Crying*] I don't know what possessed me, Joe, but I wish you hadn't taught me to call Knaves at cards Jacks.

JOE. Pip, lies is lies. Don't you tell no more of 'em, Pip. That ain't the way to get out of being common, old chap. You are oncommon in some things. You're a oncommon scholar.

PIP. I have learnt next to nothing, Joe. You think much of me. It's only that.

JOE. Well, Pip, be it so or be it son't, you must be a common scholar afore you can be a oncommon one! The king upon his throne, can't sit and write his acts of Parliament without having begun, when he were a unpromoted Prince, with the alphabet—and begun at A too, and worked his way to Z. And I know what that is to do, though I can't say I've exactly done it.

PIP. You are not angry with me, Joe?

JOE. No, old chap. But them lies were of a stunning and outdacious sort. A sincere well-wisher would adwise, Pip, their being dropped into your meditations, when you go upstairs to bed. That's all, old chap, and don't never do it no more.

Scene 12. Satis House gate.

ESTELLA unlocks the gate. PIP enters.

ESTELLA. Well?

PIP. Well, miss?

ESTELLA. Am I pretty?

PIP. Yes, I think you are very pretty.

ESTELLA. Am I insulting?

PIP. Not so much so as you were last time.

ESTELLA. Not so much so?

PIP. No.

ESTELLA slaps his face.

ESTELLA. Now? You little coarse monster, what do you think of me now?

PIP. I shall not tell you.

ESTELLA. Because you are going to tell upstairs. Is that it?

PIP. No, that's not it.

ESTELLA. Why don't you cry again, you little wretch?

PIP. Because I'll never cry for you again.

JAGGERS enters, to make his way out of the gate.

JAGGERS. Boy of the neighbourhood? Hey?

PIP. Yes, sir.

JAGGERS. How do you come here?

PIP. Miss Havisham sent for me, sir.

JAGGERS. Well! Behave yourself. I have a pretty large experience of boys, and you're a bad set of fellows. Now mind you behave yourself!

JAGGERS exits by the gate and ESTELLA locks it after him.

Scene 13. Satis House interior

ESTELLA leads PIP by candle through the dark house to the candlelit room.

HAVISHAM. So! The days have worn away, have they?

PIP. Yes, ma'am. To-day is—

HAVISHAM. There, there, there! I don't want to know. Are you ready to play?

PIP. I don't think I am, ma'am.

HAVISHAM. Not at cards again?

PIP. Yes, ma'am; I could do that, if I was wanted.

HAVISHAM. Since this house strikes you old and grave, boy, and you are unwilling to play, are you willing to work?

PIP. Quite willing.

HAVISHAM. Then go into that opposite room.

PIP crosses to another room, with a large table holding a wedding cake. Everything is covered in cobwebs. HAVISHAM follows. She places a hand on his shoulder and he winces.

HAVISHAM. This is where I will be laid when I am dead. They shall come and look at me here. What do you think that is? That, where those cobwebs are?

PIP. I can't guess what it is, ma'am.

HAVISHAM. It's a great cake. A bride-cake. Mine! Come, come, come! Walk me, walk me!

They walk round the room, she leaning heavily on his shoulder.

HAVISHAM. Slower! This is my birthday, Pip. On this day of the year, long before you were born, this heap of decay was brought here. The mice have gnawed at it, and sharper teeth have gnawed at me. When the ruin is complete and they lay me dead, in my bride's dress on the bride's table, so much the better if it is done on this day!

Time passes.
PIP supports Miss HAVISHAM as she leans on his arm.

HAVISHAM. You are growing tall, Pip! Tell me the name again of that blacksmith of yours.

PIP. Joe Gargery, ma'am.

HAVISHAM. Meaning the master you were to be apprenticed to?

PIP. Yes, Miss Havisham.

HAVISHAM. You had better be apprenticed at once. Would Gargery come here with you, and bring your indentures, do you think?

PIP. I think he would take it as an honour to be asked, Miss Havisham.

HAVISHAM. Then let him come. Let him come soon, and come along with you.

ESTELLA takes a place behind Miss Havisham's chair. JOE, dressed in his Sunday best, with hat in hand, enters.

HAVISHAM. You are the husband of the sister of this boy?

JOE. Which I meantersay, Pip, as I hup and married your sister, and I were at the time what you might call a single man.

HAVISHAM. And you have reared the boy, with the intention of taking him for your apprentice; is that so, Mr. Gargery?

JOE. You know, Pip, it were looked for'ard to betwixt us, as being calc'lated to lead to larks. Not but what, Pip, if you had ever made objections to the business, but what they would have been attended to, don't you see?

HAVISHAM. Has the boy ever made any objection? Does he like the trade?

JOE. It is well beknown to yourself, Pip, that it were the wish of your own hart.

HAVISHAM. Have you brought his indentures with you?

JOE. Well, Pip, you yourself see me put 'em in my 'at, and therefore you know as they are here.

JOE takes the indentures from his hat and gives them to PIP. ESTELLA sniggers. Embarrassed, PIP passes the indentures to HAVISHAM.

HAVISHAM. You expected no premium with the boy?

Pause.

PIP. Joe! Why don't you answer—

JOE. Pip, which I meantersay you know the answer to be full well No, and wherefore should I say it?

Miss Havisham nods and takes up a little bag from the table beside her.

HAVISHAM. Pip has earned a premium. There are five-and-twenty guineas in this bag. Give it to your master, Pip.

JOE. This is wery liberal on your part, Pip, and grateful welcome. And now, old chap, may we do our duty, both on us, and by them which your liberal present—for the satisfaction of—them as never— and from myself far be it!

HAVISHAM. Good-bye, Pip! Let them out, Estella.

PIP. Am I to come again, Miss Havisham?

HAVISHAM. No. Gargery is your master now. Gargery! One word!

ESTELLA leads PIP out.

HAVISHAM. The boy has been a good boy here, and that is his reward. Of course, as an honest man, you will expect no other and no more.

Scene 14. Gargery kitchen

JOE and PIP begin changing into their working clothes. Biddy takes their Sunday best away.

MRS JOE. Well? I wonder you condescend to come back to such poor society as this, I am sure I do!

JOE. Miss Havisham, made it wery partick'ler that we

should give her compliments to Mrs. J. Gargery—

MRS JOE. Much good they'll do me! And what did she give young'un here?

JOE. She giv' him nothing. What she giv', she giv' to his friends. 'And by his friends,' were her explanation, 'I mean into the hands of his sister Mrs. J. Gargery.

MRS JOE.   And how much have you got?

JOE. What would present company say to ten pound?

MRS JOE.   They'd say, pretty well. Not too much, but pretty well.

JOE. It's more than that, then.

MRS JOE. Why, you don't mean to say—

JOE. What would present company say to twenty pound?

MRS JOE. Handsome would be the word.

JOE. Well, then, it's more than twenty pound.

MRS JOE. More than that?

JOE. Then to make an end of it — it's five-and-twenty pound.

After a pause, MRS JOE begins to laugh. She laughs and laughs. PIP and Joe go into...

Scene 15. Joe's forge.

JOE is at the anvil, with ORLICK. PIP holds bellows.

PIP. Joe, don't you think I ought to make Miss Havisham a visit?

JOE. She might think you expected something of her.

PIP. Don't you think I might say that I did not, Joe?

JOE. You might, old chap, and she might credit it. Similarly, she mightn't. When Miss Havisham done the handsome thing by you, she called me back to say to me as that were all.

PIP. But Joe.

JOE. Yes, old chap.

PIP. Here am I, getting on in the first year of my time, and, since the day of my being bound, I have never thanked Miss Havisham. But what I wanted to say was, that as we are rather slack just now, if you would give me a half-holiday to-morrow, I think I would go uptown and make a call on Miss Est—Havisham.

JOE. Which her name, ain't Estavisham, Pip, unless she have been rechris'ened.

PIP. I know, Joe, I know. It was a slip of mine. What do you think of it, Joe?

JOE. Well, Pip, if you think well of it, I think well of it.

ORLICK. Now, master! Sure you're not a going to favour only one of us. If Young Pip has a half-holiday, do as much for Old Orlick.

JOE. Why, what'll you do with a half-holiday, if you get it?

ORLICK. What'll I do with it! What'll he do with it? I'll do as much with it as him.

JOE. As to Pip, he's going up town.

ORLICK. Well then, as to Old Orlick, he's a going up town. Two can go up town. Tain't only one wot can go up town.

JOE. Don't lose your temper.

MRS JOE enters.

ORLICK. Shall if I like. Now, master! Come. No favouring in this shop. Be a man!

JOE. Then, as in general you stick to your work as well as most men, let it be a half-holiday for all.

MRS JOE. You fool, giving holidays to great idle hulkers like that! You are a rich man, upon my life, to waste wages in that way. I wish I was his master!

ORLICK. You'd be everybody's master, if you durst.

JOE. Let her alone.

MRS JOE. I'd be a match for all noodles and rogues. And a match for you, who are the blackest-looking and the worst rogue between this and France!

ORLICK. You're a foul shrew, Mother Gargery.

JOE. Let her alone, will you?

MRS JOE. What did you say? What did you say? What did that fellow Orlick say to me? What did he call me, with my husband standing by?

JOE and ORLICK fight, with ORLICK ending on the ground.

PIP exits to Kitchen to change to his Sunday best.

Scene 16. Satis House

In Havisham's candlelit room, HAVISHAM seated, leaning on her stick.

HAVISHAM. Well? I hope you want nothing? You'll get

nothing.

PIP. No indeed, Miss Havisham. I only wanted you to know that I am doing very well in my apprenticeship and am always much obliged to you.

HAVISHAM. There, there! Come now and then; come on your birthday. —Ay! You are looking round for Estella? Hey?

PIP. I—I hope she is well.

HAVISHAM. Abroad, educating for a lady; far out of reach; prettier than ever; admired by all who see her. [*Pause*] Do you feel that you have lost her?

She laughs. She laughs and laughs.

Scene 17. A lane

Dark and misty. PIP is walking home.

PIP. Halloa! Orlick there?

ORLICK enters, casually.

ORLICK. I was standing by a minute, on the chance of company.

PIP. You are late.

ORLICK. Well? And you're late. By the by, the guns is going again.

PIP. At the Hulks?

ORLICK. Ay! There's some of the birds flown from the cages. The guns have been going since dark, about. You'll hear one presently.

PUMBLECHOOK enters in an agitated state.

PUMBLECHOOK. There's something wrong, up at your place, Pip. Run all!

They all run.

PIP. What is it?

PUMBLECHOOK. I can't quite understand. The house seems to have been violently entered when Joe Gargery was out. Supposed by convicts. Somebody has been attacked and hurt.

They burst into...

Scene 18. Gargery kitchen

MRS JOE lies senseless on the floor, with a wound to the back of her head. Joe is at the table with his head in his hands. PIP picks up a convict's leg iron (Magwitch's) from the floor.

JOE. That's been filed asunder some good while ago. Such a fine figure of a woman as she once were, Pip!

Together, they help MRS JOE into a chair. She opens her mouth but cannot speak.

ORLICK is hammering in the forge next door. BIDDY enters and starts to spoon-feed soup to MRS JOE, who gestures for a slate and chalk on the table. She draws a crude "T". They look puzzled. JOE goes to the forge and takes the hammer from ORLICK and returns with it. MRS JOE shakes her head violently.

BIDDY. Why of course! Don't you see? It's him!

JOE. Who, Biddy?

BIDDY. Orlick, without a doubt!

JOE goes to forge and brings a reluctant ORLICK before MRS JOE. A pause: ORLICK is nervous, PIP expects an accusation. MRS JOE, grasps ORLICK's hands and smiles. ORLICK is baffled.

ORLICK and JOE exit. PIP is copying from a book, BIDDY is sewing, MRS JOE sits quietly, smiling to herself. She doesn't speak again.

PIP. Biddy, how do you manage it? Either I am very stupid, or you are very clever.

BIDDY. What is it that I manage? I don't know.

PIP. How do you manage, Biddy, to learn everything that I learn, and always to keep up with me?

BIDDY. I might as well ask you, how you manage?

PIP. No; because when I come in from the forge of a night, anyone can see me turning to at it. But you never turn to at it, Biddy.

BIDDY. I suppose I must catch it like a cough.

PIP. You are one of those, Biddy, who make the most of every chance. You never had a chance before you came here, and see how improved you are!

BIDDY. I was your first teacher though; wasn't I?

Pause, PIP nods.

PIP. Biddy, I want to be a gentleman.

BIDDY. O, I wouldn't, if I was you! I don't think it would answer.

PIP. Biddy, I have particular reasons for wanting to be a gentleman.

BIDDY. You know best, Pip; but don't you think you are happier as you are?

PIP. Biddy, I am not at all happy as I am. I am disgusted with my calling and with my life. Don't be absurd.

BIDDY. Was I absurd? I am sorry for that; I didn't mean to be. I only want you to do well, and to be comfortable.

PIP. Well, then, understand once for all that I never shall or can be anything but miserable unless I can lead a very different sort of life from the life I lead now.

BIDDY. That's a pity!

PIP. If I could have been but half as fond of the forge as I was when I was little. Joe and I would perhaps have gone partners, and I might even have grown up to keep company with you, and we might have sat here, quite different people. I should have been good enough for you; shouldn't I, Biddy?

BIDDY. Yes, I am not over-particular.

PIP. Instead of that see how I am going on. What would it signify to me, being coarse and common, if nobody had told me so!

BIDDY. It was neither a very true nor a very polite thing to say. Who said it?

PIP. The beautiful young lady at Miss Havisham's. I want to be a gentleman on her account.

BIDDY. Do you want to be a gentleman, to spite her or to gain her over?

PIP. I don't know.

BIDDY. Because, if it is to spite her, I should think—but you know best—that might be better and more independently done by caring nothing for her words. And if it is to gain her over, I should think—but you know best—she was not worth gaining over.

PIP. It may be all quite true, but I admire her dreadfully.

BIDDY. I am glad of one thing; that you have felt you could give me your confidence, Pip.

PIP. Biddy, I shall always tell you everything.

BIDDY. Till you're a gentleman.

PIP. You know I never shall be, so that's always.

Scene 19. The Three Jolly Bargemen

Tavern background sounds. JOE and PIP sit drinking with other men. JAGGERS enters.

JAGGERS. I have reason to believe there is a blacksmith among you, by name Joseph—or Joe—Gargery. Which is the man?

JOE. Here is the man.

JAGGERS beckons JOE over.

JAGGERS. You have an apprentice commonly known as Pip? Is he here?

PIP. I am here!

JAGGERS. I wish to have a private conference with you two. It will take a little time.

Jaggers glares at the others, who exit reluctantly.

Scene 20. Great Expectations

JAGGERS. My name is Jaggers, and I am a lawyer in London. Now, Joseph Gargery, I am the bearer of an offer to relieve you of this young fellow your apprentice. You would not object to cancel his indentures at his request and for his good? You would want nothing for so doing?

JOE. Lord forbid that I should want anything for not standing in Pip's way.

JAGGERS. Lord forbidding is pious, but not to the purpose. The question is, would you want anything?

JOE. The answer is: No.

JAGGERS. Very well, recollect the admission you have made, and don't try to go from it.

JOE. Who's a going to try?

JAGGERS. I don't say anybody is. Now, I return to this young fellow. And the communication I have got to make is, that he has Great Expectations.

Pause. JOE and PIP look stunned.

JAGGERS. I am instructed to communicate to him, that he will come into a handsome property. Further, that it is the desire of the present possessor of that property, that he be immediately removed from this place, and be brought up as a gentleman, —in a word, as a young fellow of Great Expectations.

PIP mouths "Miss Havisham" to JOE.

JAGGERS. Now, Mr. Pip, I address the rest of what I have to say, to you. You are to understand, first, that you always bear the name of Pip. You will have no objection, I dare say, to your Great Expectations being encumbered with that easy condition?

PIP. N-no— no objection, sir.

JAGGERS. I should think not! Now you are to understand that the name of the person who is your benefactor remains a profound secret, until the person chooses to reveal it at first hand by word of mouth to yourself. When or where, I cannot say. It may be years hence. Now, you are most positively prohibited from making any allusion to the individual, in all the communications you may have with me. If you have a suspicion, keep that suspicion in your own breast. This is not for you to inquire into. That secret is solely held by that person and by me. If you have any objection, this is the time to mention it. Speak out.

PIP is silent.

JAGGERS. I should think not! Now, Mr. Pip, I have done with stipulations. We come next to mere details of arrangement. You must know that, although I have used the term 'expectations' more than once, you are not endowed with expectations only. There is already lodged in my hands money sufficient for your suitable education and maintenance. You will please consider me your guardian.

PIP. Thank—

JAGGERS. No. I tell you at once, I am paid for my services, or I shouldn't render them. It is considered that you must be better educated, in accordance with your altered position, and that you will be alive to the importance and necessity of at once entering on that advantage.

PIP. I have always longed for it, sir.

JAGGERS. Never mind what you have always longed for. Am I answered that you are ready to be placed at once under some proper tutor?

PIP. Yes.

JAGGERS. There is a certain tutor, who I think might suit the purpose, one Mr. Pocket, who is in London. When will you come to London?

PIP [*looking at JOE*]. I suppose, directly?

JAGGERS. First, you should have some new clothes to come in, and they should not be working clothes. Say this day week. You'll want some money. Shall I leave you twenty guineas?

He presents PIP with a purse.

JAGGERS. Well, Joseph Gargery? You look dumbfounded?

JOE. I am!

JAGGERS. It was understood that you wanted nothing for yourself, remember?

JOE. It were understood and it are understood. And it ever will be similar according.

JAGGERS. But what if it was in my instructions to make you a present, as compensation?

JOE. As compensation what for?

JAGGERS. For the loss of his services.

JOE [*breaking down*]. Pip is that hearty welcome to go free with his services, to honour and fortun', as no words can tell him. But if you think as Money can make compensation to me for the loss of the little child... what come to the forge... and ever the best of friends!

PIP [*comforting JOE*]. And ever will be so!

ACT TWO

Scene 21. Satis House

Miss Havisham sits at her dressing table. PIP is now in his gentlemen's clothes.

HAVISHAM. Well, Pip?

PIP. I start for London, Miss Havisham, tomorrow, and I thought you would not mind my taking leave of you.

HAVISHAM. This is a gay figure, Pip.

PIP. I have come into such good fortune since I saw you last, Miss Havisham, and I am so grateful for it, Miss Havisham!

HAVISHAM. Yes. I have seen Mr. Jaggers. I have heard about it, Pip. So, you go tomorrow?

PIP. Yes, Miss Havisham.

HAVISHAM. And you are adopted by a rich person?

PIP. Yes, Miss Havisham.

HAVISHAM. Not named?

PIP. No, Miss Havisham.

HAVISHAM. And Mr. Jaggers is made your guardian?

PIP. Yes, Miss Havisham.

HAVISHAM. Well! You have a promising career before you. Be good—deserve it—and abide by Mr. Jaggers' instructions. Good-bye, Pip! —you will always keep the name of Pip, you know.

PIP. Yes, Miss Havisham.

HAVISHAM. Good-bye, Pip!

Scene 22. Jaggers' office

JAGGERS sits at a large desk. WEMMICK is in attendance.

JAGGERS. Now, Mr. Pip. You are to go to young Mr. Pocket's rooms, where a bed has been sent in for your accommodation. Also, here is your allowance and, the cards of tradesmen with whom you are to deal for clothes, and such other things as you could in reason want.

WEMMICK hands PIP an envelope and some cards.

JAGGERS. You will find your credit good, Mr. Pip, but I shall by this means be able to check your bills, and to pull you up if I find you outrunning the constable. Of course, you'll go wrong somehow, but that's no fault of mine.

PIP. Thank you, Mr Jaggers.

JAGGERS. Wemmick here shall walk round with you, if you please.

WEMMICK and PIP walk out of the office into...

Scene 23. A London street.

WEMMICK. So, you were never in London before?

PIP. No.

WEMMICK. I was new here once. Rum to think of now!

PIP. You are well acquainted with it now?

WEMMICK. Why, yes, I know the moves of it.

PIP. Is it a very wicked place?

WEMMICK. You may get cheated, robbed, and murdered in London. But there are plenty of people anywhere, who'll do that for you.

PIP. If there is bad blood between you and them.

WEMMICK. O! I don't know about bad blood. They'll do it, if there's anything to be got by it.

PIP. That makes it worse.

WEMMICK. You think so? Much about the same, I should say. Now here we are. As I keep the cash, we shall most likely meet pretty often. Good day.

WEMMICK exits as HERBERT arrives.

HERBERT. Mr. Pip?

PIP. Mr. Pocket?

HERBERT. Pray come in.

They enter...

Scene 24. Herbert's rooms

HERBERT. Allow me to lead the way. I am sure I shall be very happy to show London to you. As to our lodging, it's not by any means splendid. This is our sitting-room. This is my little bedroom. This is your bedroom; if you should want anything, I'll go and fetch it. We shall be alone together, but we shan't fight, I dare say.

They search each other's face and recognition dawns.

HERBERT. Lord bless me, you're the prowling boy!

PIP. And you are the pale young gentleman!

HERBERT. The idea of its being you!

PIP. The idea of its being you!

HERBERT. Well! It's all over now, I hope, and it will be magnanimous in you if you'll forgive me for having knocked you about so.

Beat.

PIP. Of course!

HERBERT. You hadn't come into your good fortune at that time?

PIP. No.

HERBERT. No, I heard it had happened very lately. I was on the lookout for good fortune then. Miss Havisham had sent for me, to see if she could take a fancy to me. But she couldn't, —at all events, she didn't.

PIP. I am surprised.

HERBERT. Bad taste, but a fact. Yes, she had sent for me on a trial visit, and if I had come out of it successfully, I suppose I should have been provided for; perhaps I should have been what-you-may-call-it to Estella.

PIP. What's that?

HERBERT. Affianced. Betrothed. Engaged. What's-his-named. Any word of that sort.

PIP. How did you bear your disappointment?

HERBERT. Pooh! I didn't care much for it. She's a Tartar.

PIP. Miss Havisham?

HERBERT. I don't say no to that, but I meant Estella. That girl's hard and haughty and capricious to the last degree, and has been brought up by Miss Havisham to wreak revenge on all the male sex.

PIP. What relation is she to Miss Havisham?

HERBERT. None. Only adopted.

PIP. Why should she wreak revenge on all the male sex? What revenge?

HERBERT. Lord, Mr. Pip! Don't you know?

PIP. No.

HERBERT. Dear me! It's quite a story, and shall be saved till dinnertime. Will you do me the favour to begin at once to call me by my Christian name, Herbert?

PIP. Happily! My Christian name is Philip and my father's family name being Pirrip, my infant tongue could make of both names nothing longer or more explicit than Pip. So, I called myself Pip, and came to be called Pip.

HERBERT. I don't take to Philip, for it sounds like a moral boy who was so avaricious that he locked up his cake till the mice ate it. Would you mind Handel for a familiar name? There's a charming piece of music by Handel, called the Harmonious Blacksmith. We are so harmonious, and you have been a blacksmith...

PIP. I should like it very much.

A waiter enters with dinner.

HERBERT. Then, my dear Handel, here is the dinner.

PIP. Then, my dear Herbert, you promised the story of Miss Havisham.

They start to eat. Pip gobbles his food.

HERBERT. Let me introduce the topic, Handel, by mentioning that in London it is not the custom to put the knife in the mouth, —for fear of accidents,—and that while the fork is reserved for that use, it is not put further in than necessary. It is scarcely worth mentioning, only it's as well to do as other people do.

A beat. They laugh.

HERBERT. Now, Miss Havisham was a spoilt child. Her mother died when she was a baby. Her father was a country gentleman, and was a brewer. It is indisputable that while you cannot possibly be genteel and bake, you may be as genteel as never was and brew.

PIP. Yet a gentleman may not keep a public house; may he?

HERBERT. Not on any account, but a public house may keep a gentleman. Well! Mr. Havisham was very rich and very proud. So was his daughter. Take another glass of wine, and excuse my mentioning that society as a body does not expect one to be so strictly conscientious in emptying one's glass, as to turn it bottom upwards with the rim on one's nose.

PIP. Thank you.

In another part of the stage, HAVISHAM and COMPEYSON enter and act out the story as is told.

HERBERT. Not at all. Miss Havisham was now an heiress, and a great match. Now, there appeared upon the scene a certain man, who courted Miss Havisham. This man pursued Miss Havisham closely, and professed to be devoted to her, and she passionately loved him. He got great sums of money from her. Your guardian, Mr Jaggers, was not at that time in Miss Havisham's counsels, and she was too haughty and too much in love to be advised by anyone.

PIP. And the man?

HERBERT. The marriage day was fixed, the wedding dresses were bought, the wedding guests were invited. The day came, but not the bridegroom. He wrote her a letter—

PIP. Which she received when she was dressing for her marriage? At twenty minutes to nine?

HERBERT. At the hour and minute, at which she stopped all the clocks. She laid the whole place waste and has never since looked upon the light of day.

PIP. Is that all the story?

HERBERT. All I know of it.

PIP. I wonder he didn't marry her and get all the property.

HERBERT. He may have been married already. Mind! I don't know that.

PIP. Is he alive now?

HERBERT. I don't know.

PIP. You said just now that Estella was not related to Miss Havisham, but adopted. When adopted?

HERBERT. There has always been an Estella, since I have heard of a Miss Havisham. I know no more. And now, Handel, all that I know about Miss Havisham, you know.

Scene 25. Jaggers' office

PIP. If I could buy the furniture now hired for me and one or two other little things, I should be quite at home there.

JAGGERS. Go it! I told you you'd get on. Well! How much do you want? Fifty pounds?

PIP. O, not nearly so much.

JAGGERS. Five pounds?

PIP. O, more than that.

JAGGERS. More than that, eh! How much more?

PIP. It is so difficult to fix a sum.

JAGGERS. Let's get at it. Twice five; will that do? Four times five; will that do?

PIP. That would do handsomely.

JAGGERS. Four times five will do handsomely, will it? Now, what do you make of four times five?

PIP. I suppose you make it twenty pounds.

JAGGERS. Wemmick! Take Mr. Pip's written order, and pay him twenty pounds.

JAGGERS exits and PIP passes into the outer office, where WEMMICK gives him £20.

PIP. I hardly know what to make of Mr. Jaggers' manner.

WEMMICK. Tell him that, and he'll take it as a compliment; he don't mean that you should know what to make of it. —Oh! it's not personal; it's only professional.

PIP. I suppose he is very skilful?

WEMMICK. Deep as Australia. If there was anything deeper, he'd be it. So, you haven't dined with Mr. Jaggers yet?

PIP. Not yet.

WEMMICK. I expect you'll have an invitation to-morrow. He's going to ask your pals, too. Mr. Pocket and

Mr. Drummle is it?

PIP. Bentley Drummle? He is so sulky a fellow.

WEMMICK. Never mind, Mr. Jaggers'll give you wine, and good wine. And now I'll tell you something. When you go to dine with Mr. Jaggers, look at his housekeeper.

PIP. Shall I see something very uncommon?

WEMMICK. You'll see a wild beast tamed. Not so very uncommon, you'll tell me. I reply, that depends on the original wildness of the beast, and the amount of taming. It won't lower your opinion of Mr. Jaggers' powers. Keep your eye on it.

Scene 26. Jaggers' dining room

JAGGERS welcomes PIP, HERBERT, DRUMMLE. Molly takes their hats then serves them wine during the following.

JAGGERS. Who's the spider? The sulky fellow?

PIP. That's Bentley Drummle. He's next heir but one to a baronetcy.

JAGGERS. Bentley Drummle is his name, is it? I hear you all row together?

PIP. Yes, Herbert and I share a boat.

JAGGERS. And do you race?

HERBERT. Certainly. Drummle always comes up behind of a night in that slow amphibious way of his.

DRUMMLE. As to skill I am more than your master.

HERBERT. Really?

DRUMMLE. Yes, and as to strength I could scatter you

like chaff.

DRUMMLE flexes his arm, inviting JAGGERS to feel his bicep. The others cluster round, flexing their arms too. JAGGERS grabs MOLLY's arm.

JAGGERS. If you talk of strength, I'll show you a wrist. Molly, let them see your wrist.

MOLLY. Master, don't.

JAGGERS. Molly, let them see your wrist.

MOLLY. Master, please!

JAGGERS. Molly, let them see both your wrists. Show them. Come!

MOLLY reluctantly turns both wrists up as the young men gather round.

JAGGERS. There's power here. Very few men have the power that this woman has. It's remarkable what mere force of grip there is in these hands. That'll do, Molly you have been admired, and can go. Mr. Drummle, I drink to you.

DRUMMLE. Not just stronger, but wiser. These others are too free with their money.

PIP. That comes with a bad grace from you, to whom Startop lent money but a week or so before.

DRUMMLE. Well, he'll be paid.

PIP. I don't mean to imply that he won't, but it might make you hold your tongue about us and our money, I should think.

DRUMMLE. You should think! Oh Lord!

PIP. I dare say, that you wouldn't lend money to any of us

if we wanted it.

DRUMMLE. You are right; I wouldn't lend one of you a sixpence. I wouldn't lend anybody a sixpence.

PIP. Rather mean to borrow under those circumstances, I should say.

DRUMMLE. You should say. Oh Lord! You can go to the devil and shake yourselves.

HERBERT. Surely, Bentley, you can be a little more agreeable?

DRUMMLE raises his empty glass with the intention of hitting HERBERT with it. JAGGERS deftly takes it from his hand.

JAGGERS. Gentlemen, I am exceedingly sorry to announce that it's half past nine.

The young men say goodnight, and collecting their hats from Molly, exit. PIP immediately returns.

PIP. I am sorry that anything disagreeable should have occurred. I hope you will not blame me much.

JAGGERS. Pooh! It's nothing, Pip. I like that Drummle though.

PIP. I am glad you like him, sir, but I don't.

JAGGERS. No, no, don't have too much to do with him. Keep as clear of him as you can.

Scene 27. Herbert's rooms

PIP opens a letter and reads it to HERBERT. In another part of the stage, BIDDY is reading aloud the letter she has composed.

PIP. My Dear Mr. Pip...

BIDDY. I write this by request of Mr. Gargery, for to let you know that he is going to London and would be glad to be allowed to see you. Your poor sister is much the same as when you left. We talk of you in the kitchen every night and wonder what you are saying and doing. No more, dear Mr. Pip, from your ever obliged, and affectionate servant,

PIP. Biddy.

BIDDY. P.S. He wishes me most particular to write "what larks". He says you will understand. I hope it will be agreeable to see him, for you had ever a good heart, and he is a worthy, worthy man. I have read him all, excepting only the last little sentence, and he wishes me most particular to write again "what larks".

BIDDY exits.

HERBERT. What larks, eh?

JOE, dressed in his Sunday best, enters Barnards Inn.

PIP. Joe, how are you, Joe?

JOE. Pip, how AIR you, Pip?

PIP. I am glad to see you, Joe. Give me your hat.

JOE perches his hat on the edge of the table. If it occasionally falls off during the following, Joe replaces it, just as precariously.

JOE. Which you have that gentle-folked... as to be sure you are a honour to your king and country.

PIP. And you, Joe, look wonderfully well.

JOE. Thank God, I'm ekerval to most. And your sister, she's no worse than she were. And Biddy, she's ever right and ready.

HERBERT. When did you come to town, Mr. Gargery?

JOE. Were it yesterday afternoon? Yes, it were. It were yesterday afternoon.

HERBERT. Well, please forgive me Mr. Gargery, but I must leave for the City.

HERBERT exits.

JOE. Us two being now alone, sir—

PIP. Joe, how can you call me, sir?

JOE. Us two being now alone, and me having the intentions to stay not many minutes more, I will now conclude—leastways begin—to mention what have led to my having had the present honour. I were at the Bargemen t'other night, Pip, when there come Pumblechook. Which that same identical, do comb my 'air the wrong way sometimes, by giving out up and down town as it were him which ever had your infant companionation and were looked upon as a playfellow by yourself.

PIP. Nonsense. It was you, Joe.

JOE. Which I fully believed it were, Pip. Well, this same identical, come to me at the Bargemen and his word were, 'Joseph, Miss Havisham she wish to speak to you.'

PIP. Miss Havisham, Joe?

JOE. Next day, sir, having cleaned myself, I go and I see Miss A.

PIP. Miss A., Joe? Miss Havisham?

JOE. Which I say, sir. Her expression air then as follering: 'Mr. Gargery. You air in correspondence with Mr. Pip? Would you tell him that which Estella has come home and would be glad to see him?' Biddy, when I got home and asked her fur to write the message to you, Biddy says, 'I know he will be very glad to have it by word of mouth, you want to see him, go!' I have now concluded, sir, and, Pip, I wish you ever well and ever prospering to a greater and a greater height.

PIP. But you are not going now, Joe?

JOE. Yes, I am. Pip, dear old chap, life is made of ever so many partings welded together, as I may say. Diwisions must come, and must be met as they come. If there's been any fault at all to-day, it's mine. I'm wrong in these clothes. I'm wrong out of the forge, the kitchen, or off th' meshes. You won't find half so much fault in me if you come and put your head in at the forge window and see Joe the blacksmith, there, at the old anvil. I'm awful dull, but I hope I've beat out something nigh the rights of this at last. [*Collecting his hat and exiting*] And so God bless you, dear old Pip, old chap, God bless you!

Scene 28. Satis House gate

ORLICK opens the gate to PIP.

PIP. Orlick!

ORLICK. Ah, young master, there's more changes than yours. But come in, come in. It's opposed to my orders to hold the gate open.

PIP. How did you come here?

ORLICK. I come here on my legs. I had my box brought alongside me in a barrow.

PIP. Are you here for good?

ORLICK. I ain't here for harm, young master, I suppose?

PIP. Then you have left the forge?

ORLICK. Do this look like a forge? I come here some time since you left.

PIP. I could have told you that, Orlick.

ORLICK. Ah! But then you've got to be a scholar.

PIP. Well, shall I go up to Miss Havisham?

ORLICK. Burn me, if I know! My orders ends here, young master.

PIP takes a candle from ORLICK and makes his way through the darkness to...

Scene 29. Satis House

PIP bows and kisses HAVISHAM's hand.

HAVISHAM. Come in, Pip, how do you do? So, you kiss my hand as if I were a queen, eh?

PIP. I heard, Miss Havisham, that you were so kind as to wish me to come and see you, and I came directly.

HAVISHAM gestures toward ESTELLA, sitting across the room.

HAVISHAM. Estella is just come home from France, and she is going to London. Do you find her much changed, Pip?

PIP. When I came in, I thought there was nothing of Estella in the face; but now it all settles down so curiously into the old—

HAVISHAM. What? You are not going to say into the old Estella? She was proud and insulting. Don't you remember?

PIP. That was long ago, and I knew no better then.

ESTELLA. I have no doubt you were quite right, and I was very disagreeable.

HAVISHAM. Is he changed?

ESTELLA. Very much.

PIP. Less coarse and common?

ESTELLA [*laughing*]. I must have been a singular little creature to hide and see that fight that day; but I did, and I enjoyed it very much.

PIP. You rewarded me very much.

ESTELLA. Did I? I remember I entertained a great objection to your adversary, because I took it ill that he should be brought here to pester me with his company.

PIP. He and I are great friends now.

ESTELLA. Since your change of fortune and prospects, you have changed your companions.

PIP. Naturally.

ESTELLA. And necessarily. What was fit company for you once, would be quite unfit for you now. You had no idea of your impending good fortune, in those times?

PIP. Not the least. Do you remember how you made me cry?

ESTELLA. No. You must know that I have no heart.

PIP. I take the liberty of doubting that. There could be no such beauty without it.

ESTELLA. Oh! I have a heart to be stabbed in or shot in, I have no doubt, and of course if it ceased to beat, I should cease to be. But you know what I mean. I have no softness there, no—sympathy—sentiment—nonsense.

HAVISHAM. Estella, I will see Mr. Jaggers now.

ESTELLA exits.

HAVISHAM. Is she beautiful, graceful, well-grown? Do you admire her?

PIP. Everybody must who sees her, Miss Havisham.

She draws PIP's head close to hers.

HAVISHAM. Love her, love her, love her! If she favours you, love her. If she wounds you, love her. If she tears your heart to pieces, love her, love her, love her! Hear me, Pip! I adopted her, to be loved. I bred her and educated her, to be loved. I developed her into what she is, that she might be loved. Love her!

PIP shrinks back.

HAVISHAM. I'll tell you what real love is. It is blind devotion, unquestioning self-humiliation, utter submission, trust and belief against yourself and against the whole world, giving up your whole heart and soul to the smiter—as I did!

JAGGERS enters.

JAGGERS. Shall I give you a ride, Miss Havisham? Once round? And so, you are here, Pip?

JAGGERS escorts HAVISHAM around the room.

PIP. Miss Havisham wished me to come and see Estella.

JAGGERS. Ah! Very fine young lady! How often have you seen Miss Estella before? Ten thousand times?

PIP. Oh! Certainly not so many.

JAGGERS. Twice?

HAVISHAM. Jaggers, leave my Pip alone, and go with him to your dinner.

JAGGERS and PIP make their way through the house.

JAGGERS. How often have you seen Miss Havisham eat and drink, Pip; a hundred times? Once?

PIP. Never.

JAGGERS. And never will, Pip. She has never allowed herself to be seen doing either, since she lived this present life of hers. She wanders about in the night, and then lays hands on such food as she takes.

PIP. If I may, sir... Orlick, the man at the gate.... I do not believe he's the right sort of man to fill a post of trust at Miss Havisham's.

JAGGERS. Why of course he is not the right sort of man, Pip, because the man who fills the post of trust never is the right sort of man.

PIP. He blacksmithed for Joe but he had a violent temper. Joe had to let him go.

JAGGERS. Very good, Pip, I'll go round presently, and pay our friend off.

PIP. Thank you, sir. May I ask you a question?

JAGGERS. You may.

PIP. Estella's name. Is it Havisham?

JAGGERS. It is Havisham.

We hear an echoing voice...

HAVISHAM. Love her, love her, love her!

Scene 30. A London street.

ESTELLA, reading a letter she has written.

ESTELLA. I am to come to London the day after to-morrow by the midday coach. I believe it was settled you should meet me? Miss Havisham has that impression, and I write in obedience to it. She sends you her regard.

Yours, Estella.

PIP. Estella!

ESTELLA. Richmond. The distance is ten miles. I am to have a carriage, and you are to take me. This is my purse, and you are to pay my charges out of it. O, you must take the purse! We have no choice, you and I, but to obey our instructions. We are not free to follow our own devices, you and I.

PIP. A carriage will have to be sent for, Estella. Will you rest here a little?

ESTELLA. Yes, I am to rest here a little, and you are to take care of me the while. I am going to live, at a great expense, with a lady there, who has the power of taking me about, and introducing me, and showing people to me and showing me to people.

PIP. I wonder Miss Havisham could part with you again so soon.

ESTELLA. It is a part of Miss Havisham's plans for me, Pip, I am to write to her constantly and see her regularly and report how I go on. How do you thrive with Mr. Pocket?

PIP. I live quite pleasantly there; at least...

ESTELLA. At least?

PIP. As pleasantly as I could anywhere, away from you.

ESTELLA. You ridiculous boy, will you never take warning? Now, you are to take care that I have some tea, and you are to take me to Richmond.

Scene 31. Pumblechook

PUMBLECHOOK, reading a letter he has written.

PUMBLECHOOK. Mr Pip,

I regret to inform you that your sister, Mrs. J. Gargery, departed this life on Monday last, and your attendance is requested at the interment on Monday next at three o'clock in the afternoon.

Your earliest benefactor and humble instrument,

Pumblechook.

A church bell tolls solemnly.

Scene 32. Graveyard / Gargery Kitchen

PIP and BIDDY, standing in front of the PIRRIP gravestone.

PIP. Biddy, I think you might have written to me about these sad matters.

BIDDY. Do you, Mr. Pip? I should have written if I had thought that.

PIP. I suppose it will be difficult for you to remain with Joe now, Biddy?

BIDDY. Oh! I can't do so, Mr. Pip. I have been speaking to Mrs. Hubble, and I am going to her to-morrow. I hope we shall be able to take some care of Mr. Gargery, together, until he settles down.

PIP. How are you going to live, Biddy? If you want any mo—

BIDDY. I'll tell you, Mr. Pip. I am going to try to get the place of mistress in the new school nearly finished here. I can be well recommended by all the neighbours, and I hope I can be industrious and patient, and teach myself while I teach others.

PIP. I have not heard the particulars of my sister's death, Biddy.

BIDDY. They are very slight, poor thing.

BIDDY walks to Gargery Kitchen as she talks. MRS JOE sits there, motionless.

BIDDY. She had been in one of her bad states for four days, when she came out of it in the evening, just at tea-time, and said quite plainly,

MRS JOE. Joe.

BIDDY. As she had never said any word for a long while, I ran and fetched in Mr. Gargery from the forge.

JOE runs into kitchen. They play out the scene as BIDDY describes it.

BIDDY. She made signs to me that she wanted him to sit down close to her. So, I put her arms round his neck, and she laid her head down on his shoulder quite content and satisfied. And so she presently said

MRS JOE. Joe

BIDDY. again, and once

MRS JOE. Pardon

BIDDY. and once

MRS JOE. Pip.

BIDDY. And so, she never lifted her head up any more, and it was just an hour later when we found she was gone.

BIDDY, crying, walks back to PIP, who bows his head.

PIP. Nothing was ever discovered, Biddy?

BIDDY. Nothing.

PIP. Do you know what is become of Orlick?

BIDDY. I should think from the colour of his clothes that he is working in the quarries.

PIP. You have seen him then? —Why are you looking at that dark tree in the lane?

BIDDY. I saw him there, on the night she died. He oft pursues me.

PIP. That was not the last time either, Biddy?

BIDDY. No; I have seen him there, since we have been walking here.

PIP starts towards the (offstage) tree

BIDDY. It is of no use; he was not there a minute, and he is gone.

PIP. I would spend any money or take any pains to drive him out of this country.

JOE is in the kitchen. PIP and BIDDY walk back to it.

BIDDY. Now, now, Mr Pip. You know Joe loves you and

never complains.

PIP. Dear Joe, how are you?

JOE. Pip, old chap, you knowed her when she were a fine figure of a—

JOE clasps PIP's hand.

JOE. Which I meantersay, Pip, as I would in preference have carried her to the church myself, along with three or four friendly ones wot come to it with willing hearts and arms, but it were considered the neighbours would look down on such and would be of opinions as it were wanting in respect.

PIP. Good-bye, dear Joe! I shall be down soon and often.

JOE. A fine figure...

PIP nods and leaves. BIDDY catches him in the lane.

BIDDY. Are you quite sure, then, that you WILL come to see him often?

PIP. You doubt me, Biddy? Don't say any more, if you please, Biddy. This shocks me very much.

Scene 33. Jaggers' office

WEMMICK. Congratulations, sir! Twenty-one today!

JAGGERS. Well, Pip, I must call you Mr. Pip to-day. Congratulations, Mr. Pip.

They shake hands.

JAGGERS. Now my young friend, what do you suppose you are living at the rate of?

PIP. I... I am quite unable to answer the question.

JAGGERS. I thought so! Now, I have asked you a question, my friend, have you anything to ask me?

PIP. Is my benefactor to be made known to me to-day?

JAGGERS. No. Ask another.

PIP. Is that confidence to be imparted to me soon?

JAGGERS. Waive that and ask another.

PIP. Have I... anything to receive, sir?

JAGGERS. I thought we should come to it! Wemmick!

WEMMICK hands PIP a folded sheet of paper.

JAGGERS. Now, Mr. Pip, attend, if you please. You have been drawing pretty freely here; your name occurs pretty often in Wemmick's cashbook; but you are in debt, of course?

PIP. I am afraid I must say yes, sir.

JAGGERS. You know you must say yes; don't you?

PIP. Yes, sir.

JAGGERS. I don't ask you what you owe, because you don't know; and if you did know, you wouldn't tell me; you would say less. Yes, yes, my friend! I know better than you. Now, take this piece of paper in your hand. Now, unfold it and tell me what it is.

PIP. This is a banknote for five hundred pounds.

JAGGERS. And a very handsome sum of money too, I think. You consider it so?

PIP. Undoubtedly!

JAGGERS. Now, that handsome sum of money, Pip, is your own, in earnest of your expectations. And at the rate of that handsome sum of money per annum, you are to live until the donor of the whole appears. You will draw from Wemmick one hundred and twenty-five pounds per quarter, until you are in communication with the fountainhead, and no longer with the mere agent. I execute my instructions, and I am paid for doing so. I think them injudicious, but I am not paid for giving any opinion on their merits.

PIP. Please convey my gratitude to—

JAGGERS. I am not paid, Pip, to carry your words to anyone.

PIP. There was a question just now, Mr. Jaggers, which you desired me to waive for a moment. I hope I am doing nothing wrong in asking it again?

JAGGERS. What is it?

PIP. Is it likely, that my patron, the fountainhead you have spoken of, will soon come to London, or summon me anywhere else?

JAGGERS. We must revert to the evening when we first encountered one another in your village. What did I tell you then, Pip?

PIP. That it might be years hence when that person appeared.

JAGGERS. Just so. That's my answer. You'll understand that better, when I tell you it's a question that might compromise me. When that person discloses, it will not be necessary for me to know anything about it. And that's all I have got to say.

JAGGERS exits.

PIP. Mr. Wemmick, I want to ask your opinion. I am very desirous to serve a friend. This friend is trying to get on in commercial life, but has no money, and finds it difficult to make a beginning. Now I want somehow to help him.

WEMMICK. With money down?

PIP. With some money down, and perhaps some anticipation of my expectations.

WEMMICK. Mr. Pip, I should like just to run over with you, if you please, the names of the various bridges up as high as Chelsea Reach. Let's see; there's London, Southwark, Blackfriars, Waterloo, Westminster, Vauxhall. There's as many as six, you see, to choose from.

PIP. I don't understand you.

WEMMICK. Choose your bridge, Mr. Pip, take a walk upon your bridge, pitch your money into the Thames, and you know the end of it. Serve a friend with it, and you may know the end of it too—but it's a less pleasant and profitable end.

PIP. This is very discouraging.

WEMMICK. Meant to be so.

PIP. Then is it your opinion that a man should never—

WEMMICK. —Invest portable property in a friend? Certainly not. Unless he wants to get rid of the friend, — and then it becomes a question how much portable property it may be worth to get rid of him. That is my deliberate opinion in this office.

PIP. And elsewhere?

WEMMICK. Well, you know, Mr. Pip, I must tell you one thing. This is devilish good of you.

PIP. Say you'll help me to be good then. Good to Herbert.

WEMMICK. I know an accountant and agent. I'll look him up and go to work for you.

PIP. I thank you ten thousand times.

Scene 34. Richmond

ESTELLA. Pip, Pip, will you never take warning?

PIP. Of what?

ESTELLA. Of me.

PIP. Warning not to be attracted by you, do you mean, Estella?

ESTELLA. If you don't know what I mean, you are blind.

PIP. You wrote to me to come to you, this time.

ESTELLA. That's true. The time has come round when Miss Havisham wishes to have me for a day at Satis. You are to take me there and bring me back. She would rather I did not travel alone. Can you take me?

PIP. Can I take you, Estella!

ESTELLA. You can then? The day after tomorrow, if you please. You are to pay all charges out of my purse. You hear the condition of your going?

PIP.   And must obey.

Scene 35. Satis House

HAVISHAM. What! Are you tired of me?

ESTELLA. Only a little tired of myself.

HAVISHAM. Speak the truth, you ingrate! You are tired of me. You cold, cold heart!

ESTELLA. What? Do you reproach me for being cold?

You?

HAVISHAM. Are you not?

ESTELLA. I am what you have made me. Take all the praise, take all the blame; take all the success, take all the failure; in short, take me.

HAVISHAM. O, look at her, look at her! Look at her so hard and thankless, on the hearth where she was reared! Where I took her into this wretched breast when it was first bleeding from its stabs, and where I have lavished years of tenderness upon her!

ESTELLA. At least I was no party to the compact, for if I could walk and speak, when it was made, it was as much as I could do. But you have been very good to me, and I owe everything to you. What would you have?

HAVISHAM. Love.

ESTELLA. You have it.

HAVISHAM. I have not. [*to PIP*] Did I never give her a burning love, while she speaks thus to me! So proud, so proud!

ESTELLA. Who taught me to be proud? Who praised me when I learnt my lesson?

HAVISHAM. So hard, so hard!

ESTELLA. Who taught me to be hard? Who praised me when I learnt my lesson?

HAVISHAM. But to be proud and hard to me! Estella, Estella, to be proud and hard to me!

HAVISHAM subsides onto the floor. PIP goes to her.

ESTELLA. I cannot think, why you should be so unreasonable when I come to see you after a separation. I have never forgotten your wrongs and their causes. I have never been unfaithful to you or your schooling. I have never shown any weakness that I can charge myself with. Leave her Pip. Come.

Scene 36. Assembly Ball

Dancers waltz upstage. DRUMMLE lounges against a wall, watching PIP and ESTELLA.

PIP. Are you tired, Estella?

ESTELLA. Rather, Pip.

PIP. You should be.

ESTELLA. Say rather, I should not be; for I have my letter to Satis House to write, before I go to sleep.

PIP. Recounting to-night's triumph? Surely a very poor one, Estella.

ESTELLA. What do you mean? I didn't know there had been any.

PIP. Estella, look at that fellow in the corner yonder, who is looking over here at us.

ESTELLA. Why should I look at him? What is there in that fellow that I need look at?

PIP. Indeed, that is the very question I want to ask you. For he has been hovering about you all night.

ESTELLA. Moths, and all sorts of ugly creatures hover about a lighted candle. Can the candle help it?

PIP. No, but cannot the Estella help it?

ESTELLA. Well! Perhaps. Yes.

PIP. But, Estella, it makes me wretched that you should

encourage a man so generally despised as Drummle. A deficient, ill-tempered, stupid fellow.

ESTELLA. Well?

PIP. You know he has nothing to recommend him but money and a ridiculous roll of addle-headed predecessors, don't you?

ESTELLA. Well?

PIP. I cannot bear that people should say, 'she throws away her graces and attractions on a mere boor, the lowest in the crowd.'

ESTELLA. I can bear it.

PIP. Oh! don't be so proud, Estella, and so inflexible.

ESTELLA. Calls me proud and inflexible in this breath! And in his last breath reproached me for stooping to a boor!

PIP. I have seen you give him looks and smiles this very night, such as you never give to me.

ESTELLA. Do you want me then, to deceive and entrap you?

PIP. Do you deceive and entrap him, Estella?

ESTELLA. Yes, and many others, —all of them but you.

Scene 37. Herbert's rooms

Pip is alone reading by the light of a lamp. A knock from offstage. Pip goes to answer it, taking the lamp with him.

PIP. There is someone down there, is there not?

MAGWITCH. [*Off*]. Yes.

PIP. What floor do you want?

MAGWITCH. The top. Mr. Pip.

PIP. That is my name. Do you wish to come in?

MAGWITCH. Yes, I wish to come in, master.

Pip moves aside and MAGWITCH enters. He has a dark cloak and hat. It's hard to make out his features by the light of the lamp.

PIP. Pray what is your business?

MAGWITCH. My business? Ah! Yes. I will explain my business, by your leave.

PIP. What do you mean?

MAGWITCH. It's disapinting to a man arter having looked for'ard so distant, and come so fur; but you're not to blame for that. There's no one nigh is there?

PIP. Why do you ask that question?

MAGWITCH. You're a game one. I'm glad you've grow'd up, a game one!

At last PIP recognises him.

PIP. My convict!

MAGWITCH. You acted noble, my boy. Noble, Pip! And I have never forgot it!

He goes to embrace PIP, who pushes him away.

PIP. Stay! Keep off! If you are grateful to me for what I did when I was a little child, I hope you have shown your gratitude by mending your way of life. Surely you must understand that—I—

Pause.

MAGWITCH. You was a saying, that surely I must understand. What must I understand?

PIP. That I cannot wish to renew that chance intercourse with you of long ago, under these different circumstances. [*Beat*]

I am glad if you have repented and recovered yourself. I am glad that you have come to thank me. You are wet, and you look weary. Will you drink something before you go?

MAGWITCH removes his hat and loosens his neckerchief.

MAGWITCH. I think... that I will drink afore I go.

PIP pours a drink and hands it over. MAGWITCH is crying. PIP pours one for himself.

PIP. I hope that you will not think I spoke harshly to you just now, and I am sorry for it if I did. I wish you well and happy! How are you living?

MAGWITCH. I've been a sheep-farmer, stockbreeder, other trades besides, away in the new world, many a thousand mile of stormy water off from this.

PIP. I hope you have done well?

MAGWITCH. I've done wonderfully well. There's others went out alonger me as has done well too, but no man has done nigh as well as me.

PIP. I am glad to hear it. I too, have done well.

MAGWITCH. May I make so bold as ask you how you have done well, since you and me was out on them lone shivering marshes?

PIP. I... have been chosen to succeed to some property.

MAGWITCH. Might a mere warmint ask what property?

PIP. I don't know.

MAGWITCH. Might a mere warmint ask whose property?

PIP. I don't know.

MAGWITCH. Could I make a guess, I wonder, at your income since you come of age! As to the first figure now. Five?

PIP sinks into a chair.

MAGWITCH. Concerning a guardian, or such-like, whiles you was a minor. Some lawyer, maybe. As to the first letter of that lawyer's name now. Would it be J?

PIP puts his head in his hands.

MAGWITCH. Put it, as the employer of that lawyer whose name begun with a J, and might be Jaggers, —put it as he had come over sea, and had wanted to come to you. Yes, Pip, dear boy, I've made a gentleman on you! It's me wot has done it! I swore, sure as ever I earned a guinea, that guinea should go to you. I swore, sure as ever I got rich, you should get rich. I lived rough, that you should live smooth; I worked hard, that you should be above work. I tell it, fur you to know as that there hunted dunghill dog wot you kep life in, got his head so high that he could make a gentleman, —and, Pip, you're him!

MAGWITCH shakes PIP by the shoulders.

MAGWITCH. Don't you mind talking, Pip. You ain't looked slowly forward to this as I have; you wosn't prepared for this as I wos. But didn't you never think it might be me?

PIP. O no, no, no! Never, never!

MAGWITCH. Well, you see it wos me, and single-handed. Never a soul in it but my own self and Mr. Jaggers.

PIP. Was there no one else?

MAGWITCH. No, who else should there be? And, dear boy, how good looking you have growed! Isn't there bright eyes somewheres, wot you love the thoughts on?

PIP. [*whispering*] O Estella, Estella!

MAGWITCH. They shall be yourn, dear boy, if money can buy 'em. Let me finish wot I was a telling you, dear boy. I got money left me by my master which died, and got my liberty and went for myself. In every single thing I went for, I went for you. And I held steady afore my mind that I would for certain come one day and see my boy, and make myself known to him. It warn't easy, Pip, for me to leave them parts, nor safe. But I held to it, for I was determined. Dear boy, I done it! Where will you put me?

PIP. To sleep?

MAGWITCH. Yes. And to sleep long and sound, for I've been sea-tossed and sea-washed, months and months.

PIP. [*standing*]. My friend and companion is absent; you must have his room.

MAGWITCH. He won't come back to-morrow; will he?

PIP. No, not to-morrow.

MAGWITCH. Because, look'ee here, dear boy, caution is necessary.

PIP. How do you mean? Caution?

MAGWITCH. By God, it's Death!

PIP. What's death?

MAGWITCH. I was sent for life. It's death to come back.

There's been overmuch coming back of late years, and I should of a certainty be hanged if took.

Cannon sound.

ACT THREE

Scene 38. Herbert's rooms. Morning.

Cannon sound. Pip and Magwitch.

PIP. I do not even know by what name to call you. You assumed some name, I suppose, on board ship?

MAGWITCH. Yes, dear boy. I took the name of Provis.

PIP. What is your real name?

MAGWITCH. Magwitch, chrisen'd Abel.

PIP. Are you known in London?

MAGWITCH. I hope not!

PIP. Were you—tried—in London?

MAGWITCH. Which time?

PIP. The last time.

MAGWITCH. First knowed Mr. Jaggers that way. Jaggers was for me. And what I done is worked out and paid for!

He takes PIP by the hands.

MAGWITCH. And this is the gentleman what I made! It does me good fur to look at you, Pip.

PIP. Stop! I want to know what is to be done. I want to know how you are to be kept out of danger, how long you are going to stay.

MAGWITCH. Well, dear boy, the danger ain't so great. Without I was informed agen, the danger ain't so much to signify. There's Jaggers, and there's Wemmick, and there's you. Who else is there to inform?

PIP. And how long do you remain? Last night you said it was death.

MAGWITCH. How long? I'm not a-going back. I've come for good. Pip, I'm here because I've meant it by you, years and years. I'm a old bird now, as has dared all manner of traps since first he was fledged, and I'm not afeerd to perch upon a scarecrow. If there's Death hid inside of it, there is, and let him come out, and I'll face him.

Scene 39. Street, outside Herbert's rooms

PIP. Excuse me, watchman.

WATCHMAN. Sir?

PIP. Did you see any gentlemen come in at this gate late last night?

WATCHMAN. The night being so bad, sir, uncommon few have come in at my gate. I don't call to mind another since about eleven o'clock, when a stranger asked for you.

PIP. My... uncle. Yes.

WATCHMAN. You saw him, sir?

PIP. Yes. Oh yes.

WATCHMAN. Likewise, the person with him?

PIP. Person with him!

WATCHMAN. I judged the person to be with him. The person stopped, when your uncle stopped to make inquiry of me, and the person took this way when he took this way.

PIP. What sort of person?

WATCHMAN. I did not particularly notice; I should say a working person; to the best of my belief, he had a dust-coloured kind of clothes on, under a dark coat.

PIP. I see. Thank you.

PIP tips WATCHMAN a coin.

Scene 40. Jaggers' Office

JAGGERS. Now, Pip, be careful.

PIP. I will, sir.

JAGGERS. Don't commit yourself and don't commit anyone. You understand—anyone! Don't tell me anything: I don't want to know anything; I am not curious.

PIP. I merely want, Mr. Jaggers, to assure myself that what I have been told is true.

JAGGERS. But did you say 'told' or 'informed'? Told would imply verbal communication. You can't have verbal communication with a man in New South Wales, you know.

PIP. I will say, informed, Mr. Jaggers.

JAGGERS. Good.

PIP. I have been informed, by a person named Abel Magwitch, that he is the benefactor so long unknown to me.

JAGGERS. That is the man, in New South Wales.

PIP. I am not so unreasonable, sir, as to think you at all responsible for my mistakes and wrong conclusions; but I always supposed it was Miss Havisham.

JAGGERS. As you say, Pip, I am not at all responsible for

that.

PIP. And yet it looked so like it, sir.

JAGGERS. Not a particle of evidence, Pip. Take nothing on its looks; take everything on evidence. There's no better rule.

PIP. Quite, sir.

JAGGERS. I communicated to Magwitch—in New South Wales—when he first wrote to me—from New South Wales—the caution that he was not at all likely to obtain a pardon; and that his presenting himself in this country would be rendering him liable to the extreme penalty of the law. I have been informed by Wemmick, that he has received a letter from a colonist of the name of Purvis, or—

PIP. Provis.

JAGGERS. Or Provis—thank you, Pip. A letter, asking for the particulars of your address, on behalf of Magwitch. Wemmick sent him the particulars. Probably it is through Provis that you have received the explanation of Magwitch?

PIP. It came through Provis.

JAGGERS. [*Nodding*] In writing by post to Magwitch—in New South Wales—or in communicating with him through Provis, have the goodness to mention that the particulars of our long account shall be sent to you, together with the balance; for there is still a balance remaining. Glad to have seen you. Good day, Pip!

Scene 41. Herbert's rooms. Evening

MAGWITCH starts up, knife in hand.

PIP. Quiet! It's Herbert!

HERBERT enters, breezily.

HERBERT. Handel, my dear fellow, how are you? I seem to have been gone a twelvemonth! Handel, my—Halloa! I beg your pardon.

PIP. Herbert, my dear friend, something very strange has happened. This is—a visitor of mine.

MAGWITCH. It's all right, dear boy! [*Hands HERBERT a small black book*]. Take it in your right hand. Lord strike you dead on the spot, if ever you split in any way sumever! Kiss it!

PIP. Do as he wishes.

HERBERT kisses the book.

MAGWITCH. Now you're on your oath, you know!

PIP. Herbert, this is Mr. Mag— Mr. Provis. He is my benefactor.

HERBERT. I see.

MAGWITCH. Dear boy and Pip's comrade. I am not a going fur to tell you my life like a story-book. I'll put it at once into a mouthful of English. In jail and out of jail, in jail and out of jail. There, you've got it. That's my life to such times as I got shipped off, arter Pip stood my friend. And look'ee here! Wotever I done is worked out and paid for.

HERBERT. So be it.

MAGWITCH. I've been done everything to, pretty well— except hanged. I've been locked up as much as a silver tea-kittle. I first become aware of myself a thieving turnips for my living. This is the way it was, when I was a ragged little

82

creetur. Tramping, begging, thieving, working sometimes when I could, a bit of a poacher, a bit of a labourer, a bit of most things that don't pay and lead to trouble. I got to be a man. At Epsom races, a matter of over twenty years ago, I got acquainted wi' a man whose skull I'd crack wi' a poker, if I'd got it here. His name was Compeyson; and that's the man, dear boy, what you see me a pounding in the ditch.

HERBERT. Compeyson?

MAGWITCH. Compeyson. He set up fur a gentleman and he'd been to a public boarding-school and had learning.

HERBERT [*to PIP*]. Compeyson is the man who professed to be Miss Havisham's lover!

COMPEYSON appears in another part of the stage.

COMPEYSON. To judge from appearances, you're out of luck.

MAGWITCH, putting on a battered old hat and losing some years, crosses to him.

MAGWITCH. Yes, master, and I've never been in it much.

COMPEYSON. Luck changes. Perhaps yours is going to change.

MAGWITCH. I hope it may be so. There's room.

COMPEYSON. What can you do?

MAGWITCH. Eat and drink, if you'll find the materials.

COMPEYSON [*Laughing*]. Here is five shillings. Come back tomorrow and ask for Mr. Compeyson and you shall be my man and partner.

MAGWITCH [*to PIP*]. Compeyson's business was swindling, forging and such-like. He'd no more heart than a iron file. I was always in debt to him, always under his thumb, always a getting into danger. At last, me and Compeyson was both committed for felony, —on a charge of putting stolen notes in circulation.

COMPEYSON. Separate defences, no communication.

MAGWITCH. And when the verdict come, warn't it Compeyson as was recommended to mercy on account of good character and bad company, and giving up all the information he could agen me, and warn't it me as got never a word but Guilty? [*to COMPEYSON*] Once out of this court, I'll smash that face of yourn!'

COMPEYSON. Your honour, you see how I need to be protected?

MAGWITCH. And when we're sentenced, ain't it him as gets seven year, and me fourteen, and ain't it him as the Judge is sorry for, because he might a done so well, and ain't it me as the Judge perceives to be a old offender of wiolent passion, likely to come to worse?

COMPEYSON and MAGWITCH exit separately.

PIP. What is to be done, Herbert? He is so unknown to me, except as the miserable wretch who terrified me two days in my childhood! Nothing has been in my thoughts so distinctly as his putting himself in the way of being taken.

HERBERT. The first and the main thing to be done is to get him out of England. You will have to go with him, and then he may be induced to go.

PIP. Yes. But, before I can go abroad, I must see both Estella and Miss Havisham.

Scene 42. Satis House gate

PIP arrives as DRUMMLE is leaving. Their animosity is apparent.

DRUMMLE. You have just come down?

PIP. Yes.

DRUMMLE. Beastly place. Your part of the country, I think?

PIP. Yes. Do you stay here long?

DRUMMLE. Can't say. Do you?

PIP. Can't say.

DRUMMLE. Large tract of marshes about here, I believe?

PIP. Yes. What of that?

DRUMMLE. I am going out for a ride in the saddle. I mean to explore those marshes for amusement. Out-of-the-way villages there, they tell me. Curious little public-houses—and smithies—and that.

PIP. Yes.

DRUMMLE. The lady won't ride to-day; the weather won't do. But I will dine at the lady's.

PIP. Mr. Drummle, I did not seek this conversation, and I don't think it an agreeable one.

DRUMMLE. I am sure it's not.

PIP. And therefore, with your leave, I will suggest that we hold no kind of communication in future.

DRUMMLE. Quite my opinion. But don't lose your temper. Haven't you lost enough without that?

PIP. What do you mean, sir?

DRUMMLE *laughs and exits.*

Scene 43. Satis House

HAVISHAM *sits,* ESTELLA *knits (or embroiders)*

HAVISHAM. And what wind blows you here, Pip?

PIP. Miss Havisham, I am as unhappy as you can ever have meant me to be. I have found out who my patron is. It is not a fortunate discovery, and is not likely to enrich me in reputation, station, fortune, anything. There are reasons why I must say no more of that. It is not my secret, but another's.

HAVISHAM. Well?

PIP. When you first caused me to be brought here, Miss Havisham, I suppose I did come here as a kind of servant, to gratify a whim, and to be paid for it?

HAVISHAM. Ay, Pip, you did.

PIP. And that Mr. Jaggers—

HAVISHAM. Mr. Jaggers had nothing to do with it. His being my lawyer, and his being the lawyer of your patron is a coincidence.

PIP. But when I fell into the mistake I have long remained in, at least you led me on?

HAVISHAM. Yes, I let you go on.

PIP. Was that kind?

HAVISHAM [*angrily striking her stick on the floor*]. Who am I, for God's sake, that I should be kind? Well, well, well! What else?

PIP. I am not so cunning, as that I could hide from you, that I do want something. Miss Havisham, if you would spare the money to do my friend, your relative, Herbert, a lasting service, but which must be done without his knowledge, I could show you how.

HAVISHAM. Why must it be done without his knowledge?

PIP. Because I began the service myself, without his knowledge, and I don't want to be betrayed. Why I fail in my ability to finish it, I cannot explain.

HAVISHAM [*nodding*]. What else?

PIP. Estella, you know I love you. I should have said this sooner, but for my long mistake. It induced me to hope that Miss Havisham meant us for one another. I know I have no hope that I shall ever call you mine, Estella. I am ignorant what may become of me very soon. Still, I have loved you ever since I first saw you. It would have been cruel in Miss Havisham to torture me through all these years with a vain hope, if she had reflected on the gravity of what she did. But I think she did not. I think that, in the endurance of her own trial, she forgot mine, Estella.

HAVISHAM places her hand on her heart.

ESTELLA. It seems that there are sentiments, fancies, which I am not able to comprehend. When you say you love me, I know what you mean, as a form of words; but nothing more. I don't care for what you say at all. I have tried to warn you of this, but you would not be warned, for you thought I did not mean it.

PIP. I thought and hoped you could not mean it. You, so young, untried, and beautiful, Estella! Surely it is not in Nature.

ESTELLA. It is in the nature formed within me. I make a

great difference between you and all other people when I say so much. I can do no more.

PIP. Is it true, that Bentley Drummle is here?

ESTELLA. Quite true.

PIP. That you encourage him, ride out with him, and that he dines with you this very day?

ESTELLA. Quite true.

PIP. You cannot love him, Estella! You would never marry him, Estella?

ESTELLA. Why not tell you the truth? I am going to be married to him.

PIP. Dearest Estella, do not let Miss Havisham lead you into this fatal step. Put me aside for ever, but bestow yourself on some worthier person than Drummle.

ESTELLA. The preparations are making, and I shall be married soon. It is my own act. Miss Havisham would have had me wait; but I am tired of the life I have led, and I am willing enough to change it. Say no more. We shall never understand each other.

PIP. To fling yourself away upon such a mean, stupid brute!

ESTELLA. On whom should I fling myself away? Don't be afraid of my being a blessing to him; I shall not be that. Come! Here is my hand. Do we part on this, you visionary boy?

PIP. O Estella! How could I see you Drummle's wife?

ESTELLA. Nonsense. This will pass in no time. You will get me out of your thoughts in a week.

PIP. Out of my thoughts! You are part of my existence, part of myself since I first came here, the rough common boy whose heart you wounded even then. You have been in every prospect I have ever seen since, —on the river, on the marshes, in the clouds, in the light, in the darkness, in the wind, in the woods, in the sea, in the streets. Estella, to the last hour of my life, you cannot choose but remain part of the little good in me, part of the evil. But I associate you only with the good; for you have done me far more good than harm. God bless you; God forgive you!

Scene 44. London street, night

WATCHMAN stands holding a lantern in the darkness. PIP walks into its light.

WATCHMAN. Is that Mr. Pip?

PIP. It is. Hallo there, watchman.

WATCHMAN. I was not quite sure, sir, but I thought so. Here's a note, sir. The messenger that brought it, said would you be so good as read it by my lantern?

PIP takes the note and reads the outside.

WEMMICK [*in another part of the stage*]. Please read this here!

PIP opens the note and reads the message inside.

WEMMICK. Don't go home!

Scene 45. Jaggers' office

WEMMICK. Halloa, Mr. Pip! You did come home, then?

PIP. Yes, but I didn't go home.

WEMMICK. Now, Mr. Pip, you and I understand one another. We are in our private and personal capacities. Official sentiments are one thing. We are extra official.

PIP nods.

WEMMICK. I heard, yesterday, while visiting Newgate prison, that a certain person not altogether of uncolonial pursuits, and not unpossessed of portable property, had made some little stir in a certain part of the world by disappearing from such place. I also heard that you at your chambers had been watched, and might be watched again.

PIP. This watching of me at my chambers is inseparable from the person to whom you have adverted; is it?

WEMMICK. I couldn't undertake to say that. But it either is, or it will be, or it's in great danger of being.

PIP. You have heard of a man of bad character, whose true name is Compeyson?

WEMMICK nods.

PIP. Is he living?

WEMMICK nods.

PIP. Is he in London?

WEMMICK nods.

WEMMICK. Now, questioning being over, I come to what I did, after hearing what I heard. I went to find you; not finding you, I went to find Mr. Herbert. Without mentioning any names, I gave him to understand that if he was aware of anybody being about the chambers, he had better get such person out of the way while you were out of the way. Well, sir! Mr. Herbert threw himself into the business with a will, and by nine o'clock last night he housed such person, quite successfully.

PIP. What has Herbert done?

WEMMICK. He has him in a house by the riverside. Without going near it yourself, you could always hear of the safety of said person, through Mr. Herbert. After a while, and when it might be prudent, if you should want to slip him on board a foreign packet-boat, there he is— ready. Don't break cover too soon. Wait till things slacken, before you try for foreign air. Now, hush. Here is Mr Jaggers.

JAGGERS enters.

JAGGERS. Halloa Pip. Did you send that note of Miss Havisham's to Mr. Pip, Wemmick?

WEMMICK. No, sir, it was going by post, when Mr. Pip came into the office. Here it is.

WEMMICK hands a note from the desk to JAGGERS.

JAGGERS. It's a note of two lines, Pip, sent up to me by Miss Havisham. She tells me that she wants to see you on a little matter of business you mentioned to her. You'll go down? When?

PIP [*glancing at WEMMICK*]. Yes. At once, I think.

WEMMICK. If Mr. Pip has the intention of going at once, he needn't write an answer, you know.

JAGGERS. Now, come and dine with me, Wemmick's coming.

Scene 46. Jaggers' dining room

MOLLY enters and serves wine to the men. She seems to hold a fascination for PIP.

JAGGERS. So, Pip! Our friend Drummle has played his cards. He has won the pool. He is a promising fellow, but he may not have it all his own way. If he should turn to, and beat her—

PIP. Surely, you do not seriously think that he is scoundrel enough for that, Mr. Jaggers?

JAGGERS. I am putting a case. If he should turn to and beat her, he may possibly get the strength on his side; if it should be a question of intellect, he certainly will not. A fellow like Drummle either beats or cringes. Ask Wemmick his opinion.

WEMMICK. Either beats or cringes.

JAGGERS. So, here's to Mrs. Bentley Drummle, and may the question of supremacy be settled to the lady's satisfaction! Now, Molly, Molly, Molly, how slow you are to-day!

PIP stares at MOLLY as she refreshes the glasses. PIP takes WEMMICK aside.

PIP. Wemmick, do you remember telling me, before I first came to Mr. Jaggers' private house, to notice that housekeeper?

WEMMICK. I dare say I did.

PIP. I wish you would tell me her story.

WEMMICK. I don't know all of it. But what I do know I'll tell you. A score or so of years ago, that woman was tried for murder, and was acquitted. I believe had some gypsy blood in her. Anyhow, it was hot enough when it was up.

PIP. But she was acquitted.

WEMMICK. Mr. Jaggers was for her.

In another part of the stage, MOLLY stands, head bowed. JAGGERS addresses a jury.

JAGGERS. This slight young woman stands accused of the murder of another woman very much larger, and very much stronger. A case of jealousy, they say. They both led tramping lives, and the accused here had been married very young, to a tramping man, and was a perfect fury in point of jealousy, they say. There had been a violent struggle. The victim was bruised and scratched, and had been held by the throat, and choked. Now the accused here has lacerated hands. Was it with fingernails? My learned friend has set up, in proof of her jealousy, that the accused was under strong suspicion of having frantically destroyed her child by this man—some three years old—to revenge herself upon him.

MOLLY sobs.

JAGGERS. We say these are not marks of fingernails, but marks of brambles. For anything we know, she may have destroyed her child, and the child in clinging to her may have scratched her hands. What then? You are not trying her for the murder of her child! As to this case, if you will have scratches, we say that, for anything we know, you may have accounted for them, assuming for the sake of argument that you have not invented them?

WEMMICK. To sum up, sir, Mr. Jaggers was altogether too many for the jury, and they gave in.

PIP. Do you remember the sex of the child?

WEMMICK. Said to have been a girl.

Scene 47. Satis House

Miss Havisham sits by her fireplace in the room with the wedding cake.

PIP. Mr. Jaggers gave me your note yesterday, and I have lost no time.

HAVISHAM. Thank you. I want to pursue that subject you mentioned, and to show you that I am not all stone. But perhaps you can never believe that there is anything human in my heart? You said, speaking for your friend, that you could tell me how to do something useful and good. Something that you would like done?

PIP. Something that I would like done very much.

HAVISHAM. How much money is wanting to complete the purchase of this partnership for Herbert?

PIP. Nine hundred pounds.

Pause.

HAVISHAM. If I give you the money for this purpose, will you keep my secret as you have kept your own?

PIP. Quite as faithfully.

HAVISHAM. Are you very unhappy now?

PIP. I am far from happy, Miss Havisham; but I have other causes of disquiet than any you know of. They are the secrets I have mentioned.

HAVISHAM. Can I only serve you, Pip, by serving your friend? Regarding that as done, is there nothing I can do for you yourself?

PIP. Nothing. I thank you for the question. But there is nothing.

HAVISHAM. You are still on friendly terms with Mr. Jaggers?

PIP. Quite. I dined with him yesterday.

She hands him a letter.

HAVISHAM. This is an authority to him to pay you that money for your friend.

PIP. Thank you, Miss Havisham.

HAVISHAM. If you can ever say, "I forgive her," after my broken heart is dust pray do it!

PIP. O Miss Havisham, I can do it now. My life has been a blind and thankless one; and I want forgiveness and direction far too much, to be bitter with you.

HAVISHAM. O! What have I done! What have I done!

PIP. If you mean, Miss Havisham, what have you done to injure me, let me answer. Very little. I should have loved her under any circumstances.

HAVISHAM. What have I done! What have I done! Until you spoke to her the other day, and until I saw in you a looking glass that showed me what I once felt myself, I did not know what I had done. What have I done! What have I done!

PIP. Miss Havisham, you may dismiss me from your conscience. But Estella is a different case, and if you can ever undo any scrap of what you have done to her, it will be better to do that than to bemoan the past through a hundred years.

HAVISHAM. Yes, yes, I know it. But, Pip, believe this:

when she first came to me, I meant to save her from misery like my own. But as she grew, and promised to be very beautiful, I gradually did worse, and with my praises, my jewels, and my teachings, I stole her heart away, and put ice in its place.

PIP. Better, to have left her a natural heart, even to be bruised or broken. Miss Havisham, does what has passed between us give me any excuse for asking you a question relative to Estella? When she first came here?

HAVISHAM. Go on.

PIP. Whose child was Estella?

HAVISHAM. I don't know.

PIP. But Mr. Jaggers brought her here, or sent her here?

HAVISHAM. Brought her here.

PIP. Will you tell me how that came about?

HAVISHAM. I had been shut up in these rooms a long time, when I told him that I wanted a little girl to rear and love, and save from my fate. He told me that he would look about him for such an orphan child. One night he brought her here asleep, and I called her Estella.

PIP. Might I ask her age then?

HAVISHAM. Two or three. She herself knows nothing, but that she was left an orphan.

PIP. Thank you, Miss Havisham. Good day.

PIP exits. HAVISHAM approaches the fireplace.

HAVISHAM. What have I done? What have I done?

A great flaming light springs up, apparently engulfing HAVISHAM. She screams. PIP runs back into the room. He hesitates for a moment then pulls the tablecloth off and wraps it around her, beating at the flames with his hands. She struggles and shrieks, the flames die down and he lays her body on the floor.

HAVISHAM [*Weakly*]. What have I done? What have I done?

Scene 48. Herbert's rooms

HERBERT is bandaging PIP's hands.

HERBERT.   I sat with Provis last night, Handel, and he told me more of his life and a woman he had great trouble with. Did I hurt you?

PIP. Tell me what Provis said, my dear Herbert.

HERBERT. It seems, —makes you shrink at first, my poor dear fellow, don't it?—it seems that the woman was young, jealous and revengeful, to the last degree.

PIP. To what last degree?

HERBERT. Murder.

PIP. How did she murder? Whom did she murder?

HERBERT. She was tried for it, and Mr. Jaggers defended her, and the reputation of that defence first made his name known to Provis. It was another and a stronger woman who was the victim, and there had been a struggle—in a barn. Who began it, may be doubtful; but how it ended is not, for the victim was found throttled.

PIP. Was the woman brought in guilty?

HERBERT. No; she was acquitted. —My poor Handel, I hurt you!

PIP. It is impossible to be gentler, Herbert. What else?

HERBERT. This young woman and Provis had a little child, of whom Provis was exceedingly fond. She swore that she would destroy the child; then she vanished. — There's the worst arm comfortably in the sling once more.—Is your breathing is affected, my dear boy? You seem to breathe quickly.

PIP. Perhaps I do, Herbert. Did the woman keep her oath?

HERBERT. He says she did. Now, whether he had used the child's mother ill, or well, Provis doesn't say; but she had shared some four or five years of his wretched life, and he seems to have felt pity for her. Therefore, fearing he should be called upon to depose about this destroyed child, he kept himself out of the trial. After the acquittal she disappeared, and thus he lost the child and the child's mother.

PIP. I want to know, Herbert, when this happened?

HERBERT. Let me remember what he said. His expression was, 'a round score o' year ago, and a'most directly after I took up wi' Compeyson.' How old were you when you came upon him in the churchyard?

PIP. I think in my seventh year.

HERBERT. It had happened some three or four years then, he said, and you brought into his mind the little girl so tragically lost, who would have been about your age.

PIP. Herbert, you are not afraid that I am in any fever, or that my head is much disordered by the accident of last night?

HERBERT feels PIP's forehead.

HERBERT. N-no, my dear boy. You are rather excited, but you are quite yourself.

PIP. I know I am quite myself. And the man we have in hiding down the river, is Estella's Father.

Scene 49. Sluice house on the marshes

PIP reads a letter aloud.

PIP. "If you are not afraid to come to the old marshes to-night or to-morrow night at nine, and to come to the little sluice-house by the limekiln, you had better come. If you want information regarding your uncle Provis, you had much better come and tell no one, and lose no time. You must come alone. Bring this with you."

PIP. Is there anyone here?

A rope is thrown around him from behind, pinning his arms.

ORLICK. Now I've got you!

PIP. What is this? Who is it? Help, help!

ORLICK. Call out again, and I'll make short work of you!

PIP. Orlick! Unbind me. Let me go!

ORLICK. Ah! I'll let you go. I'll let you go to the moon, I'll let you go to the stars.

PIP. Why have you lured me here?

ORLICK. Don't you know?

PIP. Why have you set upon me in the dark?

ORLICK. Because I mean to do it all myself. One keeps a secret better than two. O you enemy, you enemy. You cost me my place with Havisham.

PIP. What else could I do?

ORLICK. You did that, and that would be enough, without more. How dared you to come betwixt me and Biddy?

PIP. When did I?

ORLICK. When didn't you? It was you as always give Old Orlick a bad name to her.

PIP. You gave it to yourself. I could have done you no harm, if you had done yourself none.

ORLICK. You're a liar. And you'll take any pains, and spend any money, to drive me out of this country, will you?

PIP. What are you going to do to me?

ORLICK. I'm a going to have your life! You was always in Old Orlick's way since ever you was a child. You goes out of his way this present night. He'll have no more on you. You're dead.

He produces a heavy hammer.

ORLICK. Old Orlick's a going to tell you somethink. It was you as did for your shrew sister.

PIP. It was you, villain.

ORLICK. I tell you it was done through you. I come upon her from behind, as I come upon you to-night. I giv' it her! I left her for dead. But it warn't Old Orlick as did it; it was you. You was favoured, and he was bullied and beat. Now you pays for it. You done it; now you pays for it.

ORLICK takes a swig from bottle.

ORLICK. I've took up with new companions. Some of 'em writes my letters when I wants 'em wrote! I've had a firm mind to have your life, since you was down here at

your sister's burying. When I looks for you, I finds your
uncle Provis, eh? Old Orlick come for to hear that your
uncle Provis had most like wore the leg-iron wot Old
Orlick had picked up, on these meshes many year ago, and
wot he kep by him till he dropped your sister with it, like a
bullock.

He takes another swig.

ORLICK. There's them that can't and that won't have
Magwitch, —yes, I know the name!—alive in the same
land with them. 'Ware Compeyson, Magwitch, and the
gallows!

*HERBERT bursts in with a roar. There is a short struggle.
ORLICK runs off.*

PIP. Herbert! Great Heaven!

HERBERT. Gently, Handel. Don't be too eager. What
hurt have you got? Can you stand?

PIP. I can walk. I have no hurt but in this throbbing arm.

Scene 50. Jaggers' office

*JAGGERS reads Miss Havisham's note, then passes it to
WEMMICK.*

JAGGERS. Wemmick, draw up a check on Miss
Havisham's account for nine hundred pounds. I am sorry,

Pip, that we do nothing for you.

PIP. Miss Havisham was good enough to ask me, whether she could do nothing for me, and I told her No.

JAGGERS. I should not have told her No, if I had been you, but every man ought to know his own business best.

WEMMICK. Every man's business is portable property.

PIP. I did ask something of Miss Havisham, however, sir. I asked her to give me some information relative to her adopted daughter, and she gave me all she possessed.

JAGGERS. Hah! I don't think I should have done so, if I had been Miss Havisham. But she ought to know her own business best.

PIP. I know more of the history of Miss Havisham's adopted child than Miss Havisham herself does, sir. I know her mother.

JAGGERS. Mother?

PIP. I have seen her mother within these three days. And you have seen her still more recently.

JAGGERS. Yes?

PIP. Perhaps I know more of Estella's history than even you do. I know her father too.

JAGGERS. So! You know the young lady's father, Pip?

PIP. Yes, and his name is Abel Magwitch—from New South Wales.

JAGGERS. And on what evidence, Pip, does Mr Mag— Provis make this claim?

PIP. He does not make it, has never made it, and has no knowledge or belief that his daughter is in existence.

JAGGERS. Pip, I'll put a case to you. Mind! I admit nothing.

PIP. Understood, sir.

In another part of the stage, MOLLY appears.

JAGGERS. Put the case that a woman held her child concealed, and was obliged to communicate the fact to her legal adviser. Put the case that, at the same time he held a trust to find a child for an eccentric rich lady to adopt and bring up.

PIP. I follow you, sir.

JAGGERS. Put the case that he lived in an atmosphere of evil, and that all he saw of children was their being generated in great numbers for certain destruction.

PIP. I follow you, sir.

JAGGERS. Put the case, Pip, that here was one pretty little child out of the heap who could be saved. Put the case that this was done, and that the woman was cleared.

PIP. I understand you perfectly.

JAGGERS. But that I make no admissions?

PIP. That you make no admissions.

WEMMICK. No admissions.

JAGGERS. Put the case that the child grew up, and was married for money. That the mother was still living. That the father was still living. That the secret was still a secret, except that you had got wind of it.

PIP. Yes.

JAGGERS. For whose sake would you reveal the secret? For the father's? For the mother's? For the daughter's? I think it would hardly serve her to establish her parentage for the information of her husband, and to drag her back to disgrace. I tell you that you had better chop off that bandaged left hand of yours with your bandaged right hand, and then pass the chopper on to Wemmick there, to cut that off too.

Scene 51. The river

Sounds of the river. MAGWITCH is aboard a boat manned by HERBERT and PIP.

MAGWITCH. Dear boy! Well done. Thankye, thankye!

PIP. Do you see any token of our being suspected, Herbert?

HERBERT. None.

MAGWITCH. If you knowed what it is to sit here alonger my dear boy arter having been day by day betwixt four walls, you'd envy me.

PIP. I think I know the delights of freedom.

MAGWITCH. But you don't know it equal to me. You must have been under lock and key, dear boy, to know it equal to me.

The sound of a large steamer approaching.

PIP. If all goes well, you will be perfectly free and safe again within a few hours. Look, here comes the steamer, now.

HERBERT.   Handel, old chap. There's another boat coming up alongside us. I think it may be—

A second boat with an OFFICER, soldiers and COMPEYSON appears.

COMPEYSON. That's the man! His name is Abel Magwitch, otherwise Provis.

OFFICER. You have a returned Transport there. I apprehend that man, and call upon him to surrender, and you to assist.

The officer's boat rams into Pip's. MAGWITCH stands and grapples with COMPEYSON. The sound of the approaching steamer is closer.

PIP. Compeyson!

HERBERT. Good heavens!

Still fighting, COMPEYSON and MAGWITCH fall into the water with a loud splash. Men shout in confusion. The steamer sweeps through deafeningly and its sound recedes. A pause in which we hear only the lapping of water.

HERBERT. Can you see—

MAGWITCH surfaces, alone and gasping. Soldiers drag him aboard their boat and manacle him. He is clearly badly injured.

MAGWITCH. I lost ahold of him my boy, when we was dragged beneath the keel. My head...

PIP. Dear Magwitch.

Blackout. A bell tolls. In the darkness:

JUDGE. Abel Magwitch, you will be taken hence to the prison in which you were last confined and from there to a place of execution where you will be hanged by the neck until you are dead and thereafter your body buried within the precincts of the prison and may the Lord have mercy upon your soul.

MAGWITCH. My Lord, I have received my sentence of Death from the Almighty, but I bow to yours.

Scene 52. A prison

MAGWITCH lies on a bed, breathing with great difficulty. PIP enters and takes his hand.

MAGWITCH. Thank'ee dear boy. God bless you! You've never deserted me and what's the best of all, you've been more comfortable alonger me, since I was under a dark cloud, than when the sun shone. That's best of all.

PIP. Are you in much pain to-day?

MAGWITCH. I don't complain of none, dear boy.

PIP. You never do complain.

MAGWITCH, wheezing, places PIP's hand over his heart.

PIP. Dear Magwitch, I must tell you now, at last. You had a child once, whom you loved and lost. She lived, and found powerful friends. She is living now. She is a lady and very beautiful. And I love her!

MAGWITCH raises PIP's hand to his lips. Then breathes no more.

PIP. O Lord, be merciful to him a sinner!

Enter WEMMICK.

WEMMICK. You understand, Mr. Pip, his possessions are now forfeited to the Crown?

PIP. I understand. I thank you most earnestly for all your interest and friendship.

WEMMICK. I assure you I haven't been so cut up for a long time. What I look at is the sacrifice of so much portable property. Dear me!

Exit WEMMICK. Enter HERBERT.

HERBERT. My dear Handel, I fear I shall soon have to leave you. We shall lose a fine opportunity if I put off going to Cairo, and I am very much afraid I must go when you most need me.

PIP. Herbert, I shall always need you, but my need is no greater now than at another time.

HERBERT. You will be so lonely. Have you thought of your future?

PIP. No, I have been afraid to think of any future.

HERBERT. I wish you would now. In this branch house of ours, Handel, we must have a...a...

PIP. A clerk.

HERBERT. A clerk. Who may expand—as I have—into a partner. Now, Handel, will you come to me?

PIP. But if you could, Herbert, without doing any injury to your business, leave the question open for a little while—

HERBERT. For any while!

PIP. I first must go to Joe, for he has paid off my debts from his own poor pocket. And go to Biddy and say, "Biddy, I think you once liked me very well, when my errant heart, even while it strayed away from you, was quieter and better with you than it ever has been since. And now, Biddy, if you can tell me that you will go through the world with me, you will surely make it a better world for me, and me a better man for it, and I will try hard to make it a better world for you."

Scene 53. Gargery kitchen

PIP enters. JOE and BIDDY are in their Sunday best.

JOE. Dear old Pip, old chap! You and me was ever friends.

PIP. But dear Joe, how smart you are!

JOE. Yes, dear old Pip, old chap.

PIP. And dear Biddy, how smart you are!

BIDDY. It's my wedding-day! And I am married to Joe!

PIP sits and lowers his head on the table. BIDDY holds his hands to her lips; JOE lays his hand on his shoulder.

JOE. Which he warn't strong enough, my dear, fur to be surprised.

BIDDY. I ought to have thought of it, dear Joe, but I was too happy.

PIP raises his head.

PIP. Dear Biddy, you have the best husband in the whole world. And, dear Joe, you have the best wife in the whole world, and she will make you as happy as you deserve to be, you dear, good, noble Joe!

JOE wipes his sleeve across his eyes.

PIP. And Joe and Biddy both, as you have been to church to-day, and are in charity and love with all mankind, receive my humble thanks for all you have done for me, and all I have so ill repaid! I am going away within the hour, for I am soon going abroad, and I shall never rest until I have worked for the money with which you have kept me out of debtors' prison. If I could repay it a thousand times over, I would do so! Pray tell me, both, that you forgive me!

JOE. O dear old Pip, old chap. God knows as I forgive you, if I have anythink to forgive!

BIDDY. Amen! And God knows I do!

PIP. Now, when I have eaten and drunk with you, go with me as far as the fingerpost, dear Joe and Biddy, before we say good-bye!

Scene 54. Satis House gate

Evening mists are rising. The gate, now overgrown with ivy, hangs loosely from one hinge. ESTELLA, older, walks about. Looking at the ruins. PIP, also older, enters.

PIP. Estella!

ESTELLA. I am greatly changed. I wonder you know me.

PIP. Eleven years since we last parted. After so many years, it is strange that we should meet again, Estella, here where our first meeting was! Do you often come back?

ESTELLA. I have never been here since.

PIP. Nor I.

ESTELLA. You live abroad still?

PIP. Still.

ESTELLA. And do well, I am sure?

PIP. I work pretty hard for a sufficient living, and therefore—yes, I do well.

ESTELLA. I have often thought of you.

PIP. Have you?

ESTELLA. Of late, very often. I kept far from me the remembrance of what I had thrown away when I was quite ignorant of its worth. But since, I have given it a place in my heart.

PIP. You have always held your place in my heart.

Pause.

ESTELLA. I little thought that I should take leave of you in taking leave of this spot. I am very glad to do so.

PIP. Glad to part again, Estella? To me, parting is a painful thing. To me, the remembrance of our last parting has been ever mournful and painful.

ESTELLA. But you said to me, 'God bless you, God forgive you!' And if you could say that to me then, you will not hesitate to say that to me now, —now, when suffering has been stronger than all other teaching, and has taught me to understand what your heart used to be. I have been bent and broken, but—I hope—into a better shape. Be as considerate and good to me as you were, and tell me we are friends.

PIP. We are friends.

ESTELLA. And will continue friends apart.

PIP watches as she leaves. Then, slowly, he smiles.

End.

John R. Goodman

John R. Goodman is the author of
<u>Dogs and Cats and Other Lifeforms: 7 short plays</u>
and the novel, <u>Death, Dot and Daisy</u>.

<u>https://johnrgoodman.com</u>

Progress Theatre

Progress Theatre is a self-governing, self-funding theatre group, run by volunteers, and founded in 1946. They are a registered charity in England (no. 1182798).

In addition to a varied programme of productions in their own venue, they mount an annual production in the open air at Reading Abbey Ruins, including this version of *Great Expectations* in July 2022.

<u>https://progresstheatre.co.uk</u>

Made in the USA
Coppell, TX
04 May 2023

16420329R00069